Unfurl

by
Meghan Genge

ISBN: 1492368997
ISBN-13: 9781492368991

For Helen and Anna

Acknowledgements

This book has been a very long time in the making, so there are a lot of people who I would like to thank.

First to my parents: you were my first and most supportive readers. Your generosity and curiosity have shown me how I want to live. I am so lucky to have been your daughter. To Dave, Lindsay, Helen, Anna, Ann, Oma and all of my aunts, uncles and cousins, thank you for your unwavering support and love.

To my 'online' friends: whether we have been able to meet in person or through my blog or around a virtual campfire, thank you. Knowing you has changed my life.

To Jo, Sas, Susannah, Penny, Emma, Lisa, and Leonie, thank you for *everything*.

To Jessie, Darlene, and Jane, thank you for being this book's earliest and most supportive readers.

To Natasha Treloar and Hannah Seward-Thompson for your editing skills. I still owe you both chocolate!

To Faye Logan, Mark Davidson, and Roy and Connie Genge: I miss you with all of my heart. Thank you for helping me to believe in magic.

And finally, thank you to my husband Mark: for seeing me, for hearing me, for understanding me, and for absolutely everything you are. I love you.

Author's Note

While I was writing *Unfurl*, I often had the most peculiar feeling that I was writing it *for* someone. It was as if I was being given this book so that it would be read by a very specific person. I know that may sound strange, but the connection felt very deep and personal. So this book is also dedicated to *you* – whoever you are – with love.

"There isn't any such thing as an ordinary life."
– L.M. Montgomery, *Emily Climbs*

Chapter One

There was no doubt about it: Melissa Owens was becoming invisible. The only problem was that no one else seemed to notice. The people she worked with at her law office could still see her. The driver of the number forty-seven bus could still see her. The man she bought her groceries from could see her so well he occasionally winked at her when she bought a bottle of wine. No, this was a different sort of invisibility. It seemed to be happening from the inside out.

Melissa couldn't put her finger on when it had started. Growing up, she had often felt a vague sense of living slightly to the right of where she should be. As she had grown older, the feeling had changed to a dullish ache that didn't coordinate with any specific organ. The ache felt like it was coming from her heart, but it also seemed deeper and more sinister than a simple heartache. More recently she had discovered that her invisibility had begun seeping out of her chest. It would spread up her neck and make her throat ache, but it never left any external signs of damage.

The mirror didn't help her at all. It showed her what everyone else saw: brown hair, curling softly around her ears and neck and light brown eyes that stared back at her in puzzlement. The most horrifying thing was that, moments after looking away from her reflection, she would actually begin to forget what she looked like. Every time that happened her throat hurt a little bit more, and by the next morning she would find that another piece of her had disappeared.

A number of tests by the doctor had turned up nothing, but that was largely because Melissa couldn't bring herself to ask them to test her for invisibility. Chest pain had an easier ring to it. She suspected the diagnosis might have been quite different if she had actually told the doctor the truth. His verdict of healthy had left her feeling limp and ridiculous. Apparently it truly was all in her head.

"Are you awake?" A nurse smiled, straightening the pile of magazines on the table beside where Melissa sat. Looking up, Melissa nodded and smiled weakly. After talking to the doctor, she hadn't been able to bring herself to leave the office yet. Going back to work felt too hard and she needed to think about what to do next. The nearly empty waiting room had felt like as good a place as any.

"Can I ask you a silly question?" Melissa said, not really looking at the nurse.

"Of course," the nurse said, hugging a battered copy of Cosmopolitan to her chest.

"Can you see me?" Melissa asked and then realized what she had said. "You know what, never mind," she stood and began pulling on her coat.

Cocking her head to one side and chewing on the inside of her cheek, the nurse studied Melissa for a moment. Melissa squirmed, waiting for her to tell her that she was being silly.

"How bad is it?" The nurse asked.

"What do you mean?" Melissa sputtered.

"Has it reached your throat yet?" The nurse put the magazine back on the table and took the chair next to Melissa, who found she couldn't speak and sank back down onto the chair. A tiny wail started deep in her heart.

"Which direction is it coming from?" The nurse asked. Silently, Melissa pointed at her heart. The nurse nodded and frowned. "And how far has it progressed? Can you still actually see yourself in the mirror?" Melissa nodded. "Have you noticed anything that triggers it?" The nurse asked.

Melissa stared across the room. Beige walls, beige carpet, and a painting of a poppy stared back. The bold brush strokes that formed the poppy held her attention, and her eyes came to rest at last on a stripe of dark green at its base.

"More," she whispered, trying not to let her words free the wail. "It started getting worse when I let myself wonder if there was more to my life than all of this. I guess I am just depressed. Ugh. I am such a cliché."

"No, I'd say you are much much more than that," the nurse smiled, pulling a bright green business card out of her pocket. "Take this," she said. "They can help you." Although the spiral printed on the card sparkled, the card felt heavy in Melissa's fingers.

"You think I am crazy," Melissa sighed. "Is this a shrink?"

"No," the nurse shook her head. "Not even close." With a final pat on Melissa's shoulder, the nurse got up and headed out the door and down the corridor.

"Did you hear about Amy?" Nicole asked, lifting a fork full of rice to her mouth. Melissa was at her weekly lunch date with Nicole, Jennifer and Patti. They'd been meeting once a week for two years. Once it had been a power lunch. Now it was just lunch. Melissa normally enjoyed it, but today her nerves were frayed. She still hadn't been back to work, and the business card felt heavy in her pocket.

"No," Melissa said, playing with her food. "What about her?"

"She's quit her job," Nicole answered, her mouth full of rice. "She's decided to go back to school to be an architect."

"I had no idea she wanted to do that," Jennifer gasped. "What made her go now?"

"I don't know," Nicole shrugged. "But it means she and Leo have to move. They can't afford to stay in their place with only one pay check."

"She'll have to sell her shoes for rent money," Patti laughed. "God, can you even imagine? Amy, with no shoe budget! Do you think we'll ever see her again? Students are usually too broke to do anything."

As the others discussed their friend, Melissa sat quietly and played with her lunch, realizing that this was the same lunch and the same conversation she had sat through a thousand times. She had actively participated in choosing this life. Why could she no longer see herself in it?

Feeling ungrateful and irritable was not helping her digestion or her chest pains. Maybe the nurse was right. Maybe she did need a shrink. Nobody else seemed to notice that anything was wrong.

"Are you awake?" The waitress leaned in towards Melissa, holding a dessert menu. Still lost in thought, Melissa did not immediately reply. The woman smiled gently, and leaned forward a little more, placing the menu on the table. A glint caught Melissa's eye, and she noticed that the waitress was wearing a beautiful necklace. Hanging from a delicate chain was a silver spiral. Unable to look away, Melissa stared at the necklace. There was something strangely familiar about the shape. She pulled the business card out of her pocket and looked at it. The symbols were the same. By the time she realized that they could be connected, the waitress had disappeared. Her friends were still talking about Amy when Melissa made her excuses and went back to work.

Caffeine, Melissa decided, was going to make all of the difference. Stopping off in the staff room, she poured herself a generous mug of coffee. Stirring in sweetener, she wandered back to her office. As she took her first scalding sip, something caught her eye. Propped up on her keyboard was a small business card. It was bright green and the only other thing printed on it was a sparkling silver spiral. She could have sworn it was winking at her. Reaching into her pocket, she found it was empty.

Melissa picked up the card and looked around her, expecting someone to be standing in the office. Putting down her coffee mug, she turned the card over. Printed on the back were a street address and the word *More*. She could have sworn that the back of the card had been blank before. As she turned the card back over, the picture winked at her again. A hazy image came to her of a circle of women. Melissa rubbed at her eyes. That was it. She needed help.

Feeling shaken, she sat down and set the card on the desk in front of her. With no web address or name on the card, she had to resort to an internet search. Turning on her computer, she typed 'silver spiral' into her search engine. Over two million sites appeared. A search for the street address came up with zero.

"More," she whispered, holding the card between her palms.

"Coming for drinks after work?" Nancy asked, poking her head through the open door. Melissa jumped and tucked the card underneath some papers on her desk.

"Oh, actually, I can't tonight," she smiled tightly. "I have a few errands to do before the weekend."

"Suit yourself," Nancy said and with a smile and a wave she was gone. Melissa sat and stared at her computer screen for a moment before pulling the card out again. The address was for a place only a few streets away. Turning off her computer and packing up her purse, she hurried out of the office without telling anyone where she was going. She'd only be a few minutes. They wouldn't even miss her.

Chapter Two

Melissa walked up and down the street twice and then studied the card again in frustration. This was where it was supposed to be. Squinting her eyes at the numbers on the door beside her, she decided to have one more try. Carefully studying each door and each number, she walked back down the street. No, there was obviously a number missing, and it was the number she wanted. Glancing back down the street, she counted again, letting her eyes rest on the number beside each door until they came to the building in front of her. This time something was different. Now there was a door that she hadn't seen before. Nestled between two shop fronts, the door was dark green, and unlike its neighbours, it had a round silver spiral instead of a number.

With an easy push, Melissa opened the door and stepped inside. To her surprise it opened into a brightly lit, chic, modern lobby. Despite having no windows, the room was brightly lit and full of plants. On the wall to her right hung an enormous picture of a woman, painted to show her with her head thrown back in laugher. Melissa couldn't be sure that she wasn't laughing at her. A clinical looking counter filled the front of the room and behind it sat three women wearing telephone headsets. Signs hung like subtitles above each of their heads. One read, 'I know where

I am going,' another said, 'I just need a little help,' and over the third woman hung a sign that read, 'I haven't got a clue.'

Melissa stood and looked at the signs for a few minutes, unsure of what to do. Behind her, the door swished open and a smartly dressed woman entered.

"Excuse me," she said. "Do you mind if I go ahead of you? I know exactly where I am going." Melissa shook her head so the woman walked past her and straight up to the appropriate desk. Melissa watched her for a moment and then walked up to the desk that was under 'I haven't got a clue.'

"Hello there," the woman behind the desk beamed. "Are you here because of a referral, a hunch, or a dream?" The woman licked the tip of her index finger and pulled a form from under the counter. Placing the form on the desk in front of her, she picked up a pencil whose tip also got a lick.

Unable to summon any voice, Melissa just nodded.

"Well which is it?" The woman looked up at her over the rims of her glasses, pencil poised.

"Um, a business card actually," Melissa answered, holding out the card.

"Oh, well congratulations, but you are actually at the wrong desk. You have been referred, so you need to be in the, 'I just need a little help' line." Scribbling on the form, she stamped it and handed it to Melissa, indicating that she should take it with her to the next desk.

Melissa got in line behind two other women, form clutched tightly in her hands. The word 'referral' was stamped across the paper in solid black capital letters. Feeling sick, she decided that she should leave. Before she could do anything else, the woman in front of her turned around.

"First time?" the woman asked. Melissa nodded.

"I've been here twice, but I have never made it up to this desk before. I've always been too afraid to stay. But I just keep on getting signs that there is something more I need to do, so today's the day! Third time's the charm, right?"

Melissa didn't know how to answer, but the receptionist called the woman to the counter. With a smile in Melissa's direction, the woman stepped forward. Melissa watched her go and then stared nervously at her form, not wanting to talk to anyone else.

"Next, please," the receptionist smiled. Melissa looked around her, hoping that there was someone else waiting. There wasn't. Handing over the form, she stood in front of the counter, placing both hands on its cold, smooth surface.

"I think there has been a mistake," she began. "I'm not sure I need to be here."

"Let me just check over your form and I will let you know," the woman replied with a smile. Melissa studied her while the woman studied the form. Dressed all in white, the clinical look was completed by the perfectly straight line of the receptionist's chin-length white bob.

"Okay, so you've had a referral," the woman said, pointing with her pencil at the form. "You are in the right place. Could you tell me a little more about yourself so that I can send you in the right direction?"

"I don't know what you mean," Melissa whispered.

"That's okay," the receptionist smiled again. "I'm used to it. People very rarely know when it's time to begin. Just tell me about yourself and I will take care of the rest. Have you been having any unusual dreams?" Melissa nodded. "Any funny longings? Aches and pains? Feeling like you are missing something?" Melissa nodded yes to all of the questions. The receptionist took notes as she spoke, occasionally asking Melissa to clarify a small detail.

"Well, congratulations! It is definitely time for you to be here."

"I'm sorry," Melissa said. "I still think that there's been a misunderstanding. I need to admit to you that I am not completely sure where I am."

"Have faith," the woman smiled gently and leaned forward. "Now, we need you to begin by taking this form through that door on your left.

"Oh, I don't think I can stay very much longer," Melissa said, suddenly realizing she had been away for too long. "I need to get back to work."

"Give me your work number and I will contact them. I'll let them know not to expect you back today."

"Oh, but I can't do that," Melissa protested.

"Don't worry," the woman winked at her, telephone already against her ear. "They'll be okay with it. Now go through that door on your left. Anna is waiting for you."

Melissa's brain felt foggy as she headed for the door. The form was heavy in her hand, and she looked again at the photograph of the laughing woman. She knew that she should probably turn around and get out of there quickly, but her deepest instinct was to stay.

"More," her heart whispered.

"More," the woman in the picture promised.

Melissa opened the door.

Chapter Three

The room was empty.

"Hello?" She called.

"You must be Melissa," a voice said from behind her, making Melissa squeak. At least a foot shorter than Melissa, the woman had bushy orangey-red hair that stuck out wildly around her head and a squinty, pointy, very freckled face. Even her lips had freckles on them. Clipboard in hand, the woman looked at Melissa expectantly over the rims of a pair of square glasses. Unable to speak, Melissa nodded in response to the woman's question.

"I'm Anna. The first thing I need you to do is tell me your shoe size."

"Excuse me?"

"Your shoe size," Anna said, indicating towards Melissa's feet with her pencil. "You are going to be doing a lot of travelling and we can't have you doing it in those!"

"Travelling?" Melissa said, looking down at her shiny red high-heeled shoes.

"Oh, yes," Anna chirped. "You won't get far in *this* world wearing shiny red high-heeled shoes. They are good for sitting and showing off, but not so good for a long journey!"

"Excuse me," Melissa began. "I don't mean to be rude, but I am still not exactly sure what this is all about. Where exactly do you think I am going?"

"I don't know," Anna replied slowly. Pale apple green eyes looked directly up into Melissa's brown eyes and studied them intently.

"What do you mean, you don't know?" Melissa sputtered. "You just said…" she couldn't finish. Her head started to ache again, and she felt her cheeks flush.

"Come into my office and have a seat," Anna said, opening another door and gently pushing Melissa through it. Anna's office was bright yellow and smelled of fresh lemonade and mint. Paintings and sculptures filled the room, but it was the windows that caught Melissa's attention. Even though she knew that they were on the bottom floor in a city building, Anna's windows disagreed with her. Through one, Melissa could see a lush flower garden and through the other Melissa was certain she could see an Italian street. Between the windows sat a statue of a woman sitting cross-legged on the ground with her arms and face stretched upwards towards the sky.

"Please, sit." Anna instructed as she sat down behind her desk. Melissa obeyed.

"Is this some sort of reality show?" Melissa finally asked. "Are you going to make me face my fears or live in a house full of strangers or something?"

"No," Anna smiled. "To be honest, your journey is up to you. You've already started it, we just help you get moving in the right direction."

"Already started?" Melissa asked.

"I am going to ask you a few questions," Anna said. She sat back in her chair and folded her hands on her stomach. "Are you happy?"

Melissa felt a strange sinking feeling in her throat and just looked at Anna, unable to get any sound to come out.

"Are you satisfied with your life just as it is?" Melissa's throat closed a little bit more in reply.

"Do you feel like you are missing something?" Anna asked. Melissa just looked at her.

"What would you need to do in order to tell me an honest yes to those questions?" Anna asked, but this time she waited for an answer. Melissa gulped, trying to dislodge the lump that was sitting where her voice should be.

"I don't know," Melissa finally said. She knew deep down that she had once known the answer to that question. It must be what was stuck deep down inside her chest. She must have swallowed it whole.

"Where does it hurt right now?" Anna asked gently, sitting up and picking up her pen again.

"My throat is tight and sore and my chest aches. I feel hollow and tight at the same time," Melissa said, trying to hold back her tears.

"How do you feel right now?" Anna asked, leaning forward.

"Lost," Melissa said, feeling the hot tears begin. Shame filled her. Surely there were people with bigger problems than hers. She was fine. Flashes from her life flipped through Melissa's mind. She had experienced grief and disappointment, but who hadn't? For a moment she thought of her grandmother, the image hurting just as much as the loss had. Past choices echoed in her ears and she swallowed the what-ifs, forcing them back into the depths. Tucking some hair back behind her right ear, she looked back up at Anna. Hot tears began to flow down her cheeks and she wiped them away with stiff fingers.

"Okay Melissa, I think I have everything I need," Anna said. After writing something on Melissa's chart, she pushed a button on her desk. A woman came into the office carrying a pair of hiking shoes, and placed them on the desk in front of Melissa. "Would you like to begin your journey now?" Melissa just looked at her.

"We don't offer holidays here," Anna began to explain. "It is time for you to find answers to the questions that make your chest ache. It's time to reconnect you to your life."

"Connect me to my life?" Melissa asked, standing up and moving toward the desk. "But if you want me to start right now, this journey will disconnect me! I have a life to get back to. I have plans for the weekend, a boss to meet on Monday, and a boy-friend who will wonder where I am. I haven't packed anything. I have milk in my fridge! I can't just leave right now!"

"It's your choice when you begin, Melissa, but I can tell you that if you are willing to start right now I can guarantee that we will take care of all of those things. We will pack for you and we will make your excuses. All will be well. If you start right now, you will be able to come back to all of them stronger and more connected to your own life. You are here for a reason Melissa. You need to ask yourself a question: how badly do you want to change the way that you feel inside? All you have to do is show up. I'll leave you for a moment to think about it." With that, Anna picked up her glasses and left the room.

Melissa's head was spinning. This was crazy. In a moment of panic, she fumbled in her bag for her phone, hoping to call someone for advice. The phone beeped its denial: no signal.

"What should I do?" She whispered at its quiet face. It didn't answer, but a soft swishing noise made her turn. Behind her, three doors had opened simultaneously. The first opened into an enormous room filled with rows and rows of women sitting at desks. Each woman was scribbling on a piece of paper. It was absolutely quiet in the room and the women worked as feverishly as if they were writing an important exam.

The next door opened to the outside of the building where a van sat waiting by the curb. Through the third door she could see the lobby.

"If you still want to think about it, you'll have to go through that first door," Anna said, appearing at her side and making Melissa jump. "Those women are all trying to decide what to do next."

"All of them?" Melissa asked, walking over to look through the first door again.

"All of them," Anna nodded. "Thinking about it is the most popular choice, I'm afraid. These women are all weighing the pros and cons and working through all of the things that could go wrong before they decide what to do." Melissa watched for a few minutes and realized that none of the women were getting up and coming forward. They all seemed quite comfortable in their indecision.

"But if your heart has already made a decision then you need to choose one of the other paths. Either way you need to go now. I have other women to see." Anna looked over her glasses at Melissa.

"What do you think I should do?" Melissa asked.

"It doesn't matter what I think," Anna replied with a gentle smile. "You know that you have already made your decision anyway."

"I know what I want to do, but I am afraid," Melissa admitted.

"What are you afraid of?" Anna asked.

"Of going through this door and regretting it. I still don't really know what this is all about. I'm afraid of not being safe, of not being in control, of losing my job, of not knowing what is going to happen next, of failure. But I am also afraid of going back through the other door and always feeling like this."

"Well then you have to ask yourself which fear is stronger. What are you more afraid of? Changing or staying how you are now?" Anna watched Melissa wrestle with this question. Then, without saying another word, Melissa returned to Anna's desk, picked up her new shoes, and carried them out the door to the waiting van.

Behind her, Anna smiled.

Chapter Four

As soon as she was in the van, Melissa distracted herself from her nerves by changing her shoes. She loved her sparkly red shoes, but they were clearly not journey material.

"Hello!" A woman climbed in beside her and sat down on the seat, sighing heavily with the effort. "I'm Elle."

"Hi there, I'm Melissa." The women shook hands awkwardly. Elle was tall and thin and dressed very fashionably in a black Chanel suit. Hair the same colour as Melissa's was swept up in an elegant French knot, and her nails had been manicured with the perfect shade of pink. Elle looked like the grown up Melissa had always wanted to be.

"Are you nervous?" Elle asked, pulling a bag onto her lap and taking out what looked like a First Aid kit.

"Very," Melissa admitted. "You?"

"I'm terrified," Elle admitted. Melissa was going to ask her something else when the door opened again. Another woman stood there, smiling the most beautiful smile Melissa had ever seen.

"Hi there, do you mind if I join you?" The woman asked.

"No, but do you mind if I stay up here in the middle seat?" Elle replied. "I like to be able to see where I am going."

"Of course not," the new woman smiled. "I'm Sophia." She reached forward and took each of their hands warmly as Melissa and Elle introduced themselves. "I have something for you," she said to Melissa, holding out a lumpy, red knapsack.

"Thank you," Melissa said, accepting the gift without question. Opening her knapsack, she found a towel on the top and decided that it was the perfect thing to wrap her pretty shoes in for safekeeping. As she rummaged to make room in the top of her bag, she became distracted by the other contents. She could see some of her clothes and her journal. When had they had time to go to her house and get her things?

"It looks like we'll be travelling together for a while," Sophia said as she climbed into the back seat, interrupting Melissa's rummage.

"I'm actually glad that I am not doing this alone," Melissa admitted. Sophia smiled at her again and leaned forward.

"Oh, we'll be alright," she said with a wink. "We'll stick together, shall we?"

Melissa smiled back, feeling much more relaxed. She still had no idea where she was or where they were going but at least she wouldn't be alone. Looking back at Sophia again, Melissa thought she was the most beautiful woman she had ever seen. A sense of familiarity tickled her thoughts, but when Melissa turned around again to think about it, she realized that she couldn't remember what Sophia looked like. Sophia's strange beauty made you take her in as a whole, and try as she might, Melissa could not remember anything about her when she turned away. Every time she looked back to try, Sophia would smile so beautifully at her that Melissa would get flustered and look away again.

"Ready to go?" A woman climbed into the drivers' seat.

"Where are we going?" Elle asked. The woman was busy putting on her seatbelt and didn't appear to hear the question.

"Excuse me," Melissa said when the driver was safely snapped in. "Where are we going?"

"To the map," the woman answered, manoeuvring the van away from the curb and out onto the street. Melissa looked around, confused. Nothing was familiar. They had been in the city only moments before, but this road was small and residential with a traffic light at one end. Glancing back through the rear window, she saw only small houses and a few shop fronts. Gone were the office buildings and grey stone of the city.

"Uh, where are we?" She sat forward and leaned towards the driver.

"At the beginning," the driver said, distracted as she moved through the traffic lights. Soon the residential area was gone too. In growing disbelief, Melissa watched as they drove between fields growing thick and high with glinting wheat. Melissa looked behind them again, full of anxiety. Her stomach hurt, and her breathing was becoming shallow. Sophia reached forward and put her hand on Melissa's shoulder.

"Have faith," she murmured, her voice soft and warm. Melissa nodded, letting Sophia calm her. Beside her, Elle was panicking.

"What was that supposed to mean? The beginning of what? Melissa, could you shift over a little bit so that I can look at my bag? How did they pack all of these things? How do we know what we'll need?" Elle chattered on like this for some time. As she listened, Melissa felt herself getting frightened all over again. Elle was right about everything she said and Melissa could almost see a line of 'what if' questions streaming out of her head and spinning out through the window where they began chasing the van. Sophia tried to calm her again, but she couldn't get through the fog that Elle had created.

Corn, wheat and hay fields flashed like a slideshow past the windows. Every new crop brought an exclamation of joy from Sophia. Fields full of potatoes and cauliflower and even pumpkins flourished all around them. Sophia nearly fainted with delight as they passed by a field of sunflowers. Their faces followed the van as it passed.

"Beautiful," Sophia breathed reverently.

Ahead of them the road darkened and the fields gave way to thick forest. The trees had been cut back, but their limbs had rebelled, growing instead to form a tangled tunnel over the road. The landscape also began to change. Where it had been flat earth only a few minutes before, now large mossy rocks pushed their way out of the ground. The tunnel opened out as they came over a hill and in front of them they could see a vast expanse of forest. There were trees and rocks, cliff faces and more trees as far as the eye could see.

"Beautiful," breathed Sophia again. The others were a little bit more subdued.

Melissa rested her forehead on the window as the minutes passed. The glass was cold, but at least it felt real. She fiddled with the bit of rubber that ran along the bottom edge of the window, unable to bear to watch the trees outside, no matter how many times Sophia poked her in the back and said, "Look!"

"We're here!" The driver sang gaily as she signalled and then turned off into a small parking lot. The van stopped beside a squat, dark brown building. "All ashore that's going ashore!"

"Come on! Wake up!" Sophia said, shaking the seat. "Let's go!" Melissa and Elle looked at each other and then back at the building. With far less excitement than Sophia, they picked up their bags and worked their way out of the van, remaining reassuringly close to it as they studied the building. It looked too short to be a proper building. The walls were made of simple painted boards, and it was shingled with sticky-looking black paper. There were no windows, but there was a brown sign nailed crookedly to the closest wall. It had the word 'entrance' painted on it in yellow letters, and there was an arrow pointing to the right.

The metal door shrieked as Sophia pulled it open. Inside was a greyish blue foyer and another metal door. This one was screened and opened inwards. Pushing through, they were soon standing in the middle of someone's living room. Elle was the last one through the door and when she let it go, it closed with a bang. They all jumped and then laughed nervously at each other.

"Hello," Sophia called. There was no answer. The room was furnished simply with two dark grey couches and two large orange chairs. On one side table was a black rotary-dial phone. Thick blue-grey curtains were tied back at the sides of the windows, but thin white gauzy curtains hung between them, shielding the view. Melissa looked at the curtains a few times before she remembered that there had not been any windows on the outside of the building.

"Hello?" Sophia called again. Against the wall, on the right-hand side of the room stood a small rectangular dining room table and two chairs. On the wall above the table hung an enormous map. It was the only thing in the room that did not appear faded. Along the bottom of the map, Melissa could see the road that they had come in on. It was easy to find, as it was the only road on the map. The rest of the map was crisscrossed with dozens and dozens of lines. They all started at this building and then took various routes to one bright yellow point near the top of the map. From there they all diverged again, this time heading off the map in all directions. There were small pins on most of the paths. Melissa looked in all of the corners for a key of some sort. What did bright yellow mean? Where were all of the paths heading? She couldn't find any explanation.

"Well hello there!" A small voice called out. The three women spun around to see a small, decidedly elderly woman coming through another door.

"Sorry I didn't hear you come in. I was making some tea," the woman smiled, creating even more wrinkles on a face that was heavily lined.

"Hello," Sophia said. "Do forgive us if we have intruded. We were dropped off here, and the sign said that this was the entrance."

"Yes, yes, of course," the woman crackled. "Come in and sit down. Would you like some tea? I am sure you are thirsty, and you must be very confused about all of this." Melissa felt tears spring to her eyes at these words. Brushing them away with her fingers, she sat down on one of the orange chairs. The woman went back through the door and was back a moment later with a tray carrying a large pot of tea and some mismatched teacups.

"Now, I was expecting you a little bit later," she said. "So you'll have to forgive me for not having it on the table as you arrived!" The women all assured her that she was being most hospitable. Wrinkling into her smile again, she put the tray on a table beside the other orange chair before sitting down. Smoothing her hair back from her forehead, she began to pour the tea. Melissa watched her. Old and ageless at the same time, her movements were smooth and graceful. Her white hair was so long it touched the seat of the chair, and she wore a long navy tunic over a pair of matching navy trousers. Her feet were slipped into a pair of delicate black satin slippers.

"Will you have tea?" The woman asked her.

"Yes, please," Melissa said, reaching forward to take the cup. It was deliciously warm and fragrant. Sipping at it, she could smell ginger, and it warmed her right down to her toes.

"Well," the woman said, not pouring any other tea, and wriggling back into the chair until her feet dangled a long way from the floor. "I'm Selene. And I already know who you are. You are Melissa, right?" She asked, wiggling her feet around and looking at all of them in turn.

"Um, I am Melissa," Melissa spoke up, not wanting to be rude. "And this is Sophia, and this is Elle."

"Oh, yes, of course! How silly of me," Selene smiled. "Well, you are all welcome here. I expect that you would like to know what's going on?" The women nodded. Selene leaned towards Melissa, eyes gleaming as if she was getting to the best part of an exciting bedtime story. "Well, all I can really tell you is that I am about to send you off on an adventure. We'll choose the path that you begin on together and then you get to choose your own way along it."

"How long is it going to take?" Elle asked nervously. "I kind of left my life behind when I came out here. I don't think that I want to be gone very long."

"Well, I can assure you that your life as you left it will still be waiting for you when you get back. I can't promise that you will be the same person though," Selene smiled, one small finger pointing into the air for emphasis. When Elle looked sceptical, Selene went on. "We have been sending people out on adventures for a very very long time. Trust me. Your life will be waiting for you when you get back. It always is."

Melissa could feel herself getting sleepy. It had been an extremely weird and very long day. Although she struggled to keep her eyes open, she was soon falling asleep. All around her she could hear voices, and she swore that she could smell the forest that she sometimes went to in her dreams. Sometime in the night she felt a blanket cover her, and she snuggled into the warmth.

It felt like only a few minutes later that she was being nudged awake.

"Are you awake?" Selene was kneeling beside her, her white hair glowing in the dim light. "Melissa, are you awake?" Selene asked. Melissa didn't answer immediately, but she started to sit up. Selene stood and held out her hand.

"Then it's time to go."

Chapter Five

Melissa tried, but she couldn't remember the last time that she had been totally alone. She lived by herself, but there were always neighbours and friends and family who she could call or who she knew were there. Evenings and mornings had often seen her sitting by her window and feeling alone, but that was not the same thing. This was different. Now no one in the world knew where she was or what she was doing. Now she could not turn on the television or make a phone call to fill the silence. No matter which way she looked at it, she was utterly alone, and she wasn't sure how she was going to deal with it.

Just a few hours before, Selene had woken her up and told her to stand in front of the big map. Melissa had stood there, wiping the sleep out of her eyes and squinting at all of the lines crisscrossing in front of her. Selene had told her to pick one of the paths. When she had hesitated, Selene had said that this was something that she did not have time to think about, this was something she just needed to do. Melissa had stuck her finger out and pointed at one of the lines.

"Wonderful!" Selene had said. "Good choice! This path will take you through the forest and eventually up the mountain. All that you have to remember is to follow the path that you have chosen. Don't be tempted to go onto another path or to turn around and come back." As she was saying all of this, Selene had been moving Melissa towards the door.

"But wait!" Melissa had protested, "I haven't changed my clothes or had breakfast. I haven't got any food or a map. I don't know where I am going. It's dark outside. I don't want to go yet. Where are Elle and Sophia? I thought we'd be going together. Wait!" But her cries and protests had been completely ignored. Selene had picked up Melissa's bag and walked them both out the door. Outside the day had only just begun to lighten enough to see the woods at the edge of the clearing.

"Shush," Selene had said. "Elle and Sophia are with you. Remember, all you have is all you need. Follow the path you've chosen."

"But Selene, what do you mean? Elle and Sophia aren't here and I didn't choose any path properly. I didn't look where it went or what it had on it. I just picked!"

"Don't worry, you chose well," Selene had said, comforting her while walking with her to a far corner of the clearing. An opening had appeared in the trees, and a path had stretched forward in front of them. "Just follow your path," Selene had said again. Melissa had tried to protest, but when she turned around Selene had disappeared. In the same moment, Melissa had felt the bottom drop out of the world, as if she was on an elevator that was moving too quickly. When her vision had cleared she had realized that the building and the whole clearing had disappeared along with Selene. With trees behind and on either side, the only thing that had been left was the path in front of her. So, with tears streaming down her face and a throat full of questions and fears, she had started walking.

Livid purple bruises were forming on both arms from where she had repeatedly pinched herself over the past few hours to make sure that she wasn't dreaming. At seventeen she had taken drugs that had made her hallucinate, perhaps this was just a big bad dream because of that. Maybe she would wake up like Dorothy in the *Wizard of Oz* to find herself back in her own bed.

Melissa worked all of this through in her head as she walked. In front of her, the path was pretty clear, and it wasn't until she stumbled over a root that she realized that she had not been paying any attention to her surroundings. Suddenly she was freezing and hungry. Slouching out of her knapsack, Melissa set it on the ground and then knelt down to open it. At the top of the main compartment was her own favourite grey sweater. She had owned it for years, and it was always the first thing she put on when she was feeling in need of any comfort.

"Is this a joke?" She asked the trees. They whispered back at her, but they didn't have any answers. She shook her head and pulled on the sweater. As she bent to close to the bag again, she saw that the very next thing at the top of her knapsack was a sandwich. Made of soft brown bread and filled with tuna with bits of celery chopped into it, it was just like the sandwiches her mother had packed her when she was small. Shock forced her to the ground, and she started to cry again. Well, Selene had told her that she had exactly what she needed. She'd been cold and she'd been hungry and she'd been in need of comfort. All of those things had been packed into her bag in the order she needed them.

"I don't understand," she sniffled to the trees. "I really don't think I am ready for this. Can I just pull over for a little while?" She asked. "I'm scared." Again there was no answer. She sat in the middle of her path for a long time. Hunger overcame fear as her biggest problem, so she ate and finished her sandwich. Finding a bottle of water in her bag, she drank deeply and then just sat still, listening to the trees. She didn't know what she expected to happen, but she sat there until she was sure no answer was going to come. Finally, and with a sigh, she stood up, dusted herself off, shouldered her bag, and started off down the path again.

This time, Melissa watched her feet so that she wouldn't trip. Unsure of how to be alone for this long, she started counting her footsteps. When she got to four thousand five hundred and twenty three, she decided she was thirsty again so she stopped and pulled her water bottle out of her bag. After drinking her fill, Melissa paused and looked around. The forest was thick here. Ancient evergreens stretched upwards all around her. In their strain towards the sky, they had lost many of their lower branches. The result was a blue-green canopy that stretched far overhead, and a deep, resonant silence. The only sound was the crunch of pine needles under her feet.

Standing up a little straighter, she looked ahead again and took a deep breath. The smell of the evergreens stirred a memory, but she couldn't get it to come into focus. Cocking her head a little to the side, she sniffed again. There was something else there, hiding inside the smell of the forest: something that didn't belong. Thinking for a minute, she realized that she could smell wood smoke. There were people nearby!

Without stopping to think, she spun on the pine needles and hurried along the path. Here and there the sun broke through the canopy, sending a sparkle of light to the forest floor. Melissa barely noticed the beauty around her. All of her attention was focused on getting to where there were other people. The smell grew stronger, convincing her that she was going the right way.

If she had slowed down and paid attention, she would have noticed that the woods around her had begun to change. There were now more soft young trees, and the forest floor was populated with ferns and saplings. Maple leaves rustled and whispered in the wind, and the silvery skin of the poplars shone back in reply. It was a younger forest here. The trees were more brazen; they had more to say. Melissa ignored them, and, ducking under a low-lying branch, she burst into a clearing.

Surprise brought her up short and her mouth fell open. In front of her, beyond the forest, soared a mountain. She put her hand on her forehead, searching her thoughts for something, but she was overwhelmed and out-of-sorts. Beauty and size and scale had momentarily frozen her solid.

It was the smoke that finally shook her loose. Sniffing, she realized that she was not alone in the clearing. A small snug-looking house stood close to the other side. Smoke curled from the chimney and as Melissa watched, a woman appeared at the door of the cabin. Dressed in a grey tracksuit and carrying a water bottle, she didn't notice Melissa. With only a moments' pause to put a finger on her neck and look at her watch, she began jogging towards Melissa, eyes focused on the ground in front of her.

"Hello?" Melissa called. The woman looked up and stumbled a little. "Oh, I am sorry," Melissa gasped as she rushed down the path towards her. "I didn't mean to scare you."

"That's okay," the woman smiled quickly, checking her pulse again. "I don't mean to be rude, but I'd like to finish my run. My house is just there," she motioned with her elbow. "I'll check in with you when I get back." With that, she brushed past Melissa and ran into the woods. Melissa watched as the forest swallowed her and heard the trees start to whisper again.

As Melissa got closer to the house, she realized that her path didn't stop there. It actually marched straight past it and on into the woods. In the distance above the trees, Melissa could still see the mountain.

"We tried to go around it once." A voice interrupted her thoughts, making Melissa let out a yelp as a woman appeared beside her.

"We got terribly lost and ended up right back where we started," the woman continued, ignoring Melissa's distress. "I'm Lola," she said, stretching out her hand as if she wanted Melissa to kiss it.

"Melissa," Melissa smiled and shook the woman's hand awkwardly. "Do you live here too?"

"Yes. Natalie was here first, though. She's the one who built the house. I happened by a few years later, and she let me stay on with her. We're in training," she smiled and then started to chew on the inside of her mouth.

"For what?" Melissa asked.

"To climb the mountain," Lola shrugged, as if it was the most obvious answer.

"Oh," Melissa nodded, looking around her properly for the first time. The house was really a small cabin. A covered porch circled the house like a skirt, and various types of exercise equipment were scattered all over it and the surrounding lawn. Hula Hoops and free weights, a mini trampoline and a skipping rope all took up space in front of the house. Pairs of skis and ski poles were resting against the railings.

"Wow," Melissa murmured as Lola showed her onto the porch. "You guys have a lot of equipment!" Before Lola could answer, Melissa let out another yelp as she stepped on something and lost her balance. Regaining her composure, Melissa realized that she had stepped on a stopwatch. She bent over and picked it up, apologizing and passing it to Lola, who tossed it onto a nearby chair.

"We do a lot of training," Lola shrugged again, responding as much to Melissa's statement as to her own actions. "Would you like a drink or something?" Lola ran one hand up and down the other arm.

"Yes, please, I would love one," Melissa said, standing self-consciously on the porch. She wasn't sure if she should sit down or go inside with Lola. The house had a strange atmosphere. Even from the outside it felt like it was holding its breath. The air around her was stale and light. She wanted nothing more than to get away from the porch and back into the fresh green air of the forest.

"Come inside, I'll make you some lemonade, and we'll wait for Natalie to come back," Lola smiled timidly, holding the door open. Melissa looked back towards the forest. The trees beckoned to her, and she wondered if it would be rude to make her excuses and go. She watched the path that she'd been following disappear into the forest beside the house.

"She isn't usually very long, and you must be tired after your long journey," Lola said and then chewed on her cheek again. "Come inside." It was less of a question now and more of a command. Melissa shrugged. She was tired and thirsty. A few minutes of rest wouldn't hurt.

The air that had been standing still outside rushed inside with them. Melissa felt it flowing around her as she entered, but it had soon made itself at home and become still again. Melissa followed its lead and sat down on the first seat she found. The space was small but well organized. One wall housed a large stone fireplace, but to Melissa's disappointment the fire had nearly gone out. Above the fireplace hung a pair of snowshoes and the wall to the left of the fireplace was covered in overflowing bookshelves. Melissa forgot her fatigue for a moment, and got up to look at the titles.

"Wow, you have a lot of books," she murmured, running her fingers along one of the rows.

"It's part of our training," Lola called from the kitchen. "I'm reading up on everything to do with climbing mountains. I'm hoping that it will help us when we eventually get started."

"All of these books are about mountains?" Melissa asked, scanning some of the titles.

"Oh no," Lola said, bringing two tall glasses over to where Melissa stood. "There are some about wilderness survival, some about weather patterns, cloud formations, first aid, gear, personal effectiveness, leadership, pretty much anything that could help us when we finally get going." She handed one of the glasses to Melissa and motioned for her to sit down again. "We are making sure we are ready for any eventuality."

"So what makes you want to climb that mountain so badly?" Melissa asked, drinking her lemonade. It was so sour it made the back of her tongue tingle with pain. She smiled at Lola and sipped more carefully.

"We have to climb it," Lola said with a hint of sadness. "It's where the path leads. There's no other way forward."

"And what do you think is on the other side?" Melissa asked, gingerly sipping her drink again.

"We don't know," Lola shook her head. "I guess we'll find out when we get there. The path that you came in on is also the one that leads towards the mountain so I guess you need to climb it too," Lola smiled conspiratorially.

"When do you plan on getting started?" Melissa asked. Lola stood up and walked over to the kitchen. A calendar hung on the kitchen side of the door. Lola unhooked it and brought it back over to Melissa. The top half showed two kittens playing with a bright yellow ball of yarn and on the bottom half thick black x's covered most of the days. The twenty-ninth was circled in red. They were leaving in five days.

Lola took the calendar back and traced her finger over the thick red marking. Chewing the inside of her cheek again, she put the calendar back on the door. Melissa watched her rub her hands together and move from the door to the bookshelf. Tracing the spines of the books with her fingers, she walked its length, searching the titles and getting more and more agitated as the book she was looking for eluded her. With a small cry of triumph, Lola took a book from the second shelf and began searching through it, forgetting about her guest. Melissa watched her curiously for a few minutes. The only time Lola didn't show any of her nervous habits was when she was deep inside a book.

"Hello again!" The door opened, bringing air and energy inside for a moment. Natalie quickly closed the door behind her. "I see you've met Lola," she said. "She's a bit of a bookworm. Thinks she'll find all of the answers we need somewhere on that shelf. I'm Natalie."

"Melissa."

"Nice to meet you Melissa," Natalie said, levering her shoes off her feet with her toes and sitting down on the couch. "Are you following the path? I guess that's a dumb question eh?" She laughed and looked at Lola.

"I guess so," Melissa answered both questions at once.

"Well, you are welcome to join us when we move on," Natalie said. "We aim to leave in five days." Lola looked up from her book as Natalie spoke.

"But you guys look like you've been preparing for a long time," Melissa smiled. "Will I be ready to join you?"

"Of course," Natalie nodded. "We'll be there to look out for you. It's better to come with us than to be left behind." Melissa thought about that for a moment. Clearly there was more to the path ahead than she'd realized this morning.

"How do you know what is ahead?" She asked. "Have you seen it?"

"We've tried to go around," Natalie shrugged. "We lost the path and had to come back here. The forest gets really thick in places. We've been for a few walks in the direction of the mountain, but we've never found it."

"Never found it?" Melissa was puzzled. How could you lose a mountain?

"Well the path goes through the woods towards it, but once you are back in the woods you can't see it anymore. We've never gone close enough to actually begin to climb."

"So how do you know that the path goes over it and not around it then?" Melissa asked, looking from one to the other. Lola was biting her cheek again, and Natalie got up from the couch.

"It goes over," she said. "I need to go and get cleaned up before dinner." With that, Natalie left the room. Lola made some excuse about making dinner and went into the kitchen, leaving Melissa alone. She moved to the bookcase, running her fingers along the spines as Lola had done.

"I'm sorry, that was rude of me to leave you," Lola called, appearing at the kitchen door. The kittens on the calendar winked at Melissa. "Would you come and help me peel some carrots?"

"I'd love to," Melissa said, meaning every word. Carrots were normal. Carrots made sense in this place that she understood less and less by the minute. She could peel carrots.

The next four days passed quickly. They didn't speak again about the mountain and Melissa purposely didn't ask. She wouldn't have had time anyway. The mornings began at 4 am sharp. They started with an hour of meditation and yoga, and then they all went for a long hike back up the path Melissa had come in on. Once the hike was over they had breakfast, which was followed by time set aside for research. Melissa was asked to have a look at a book about wildflowers and to focus particularly on the kind that grew on mountainous or rocky terrain. She wasn't sure how it was going to help, but she humoured them. After research-time, they did an hour of tai chi, followed by lunch. The afternoons were spent doing various forms of exercise, and the evenings included equipment practice-runs.

"Do you think we're ready?" Lola asked at supper on the final evening.

"I think so," Nathalie said, her mouth full of pasta. They were eating a 'high-carb' meal to give their bodies enough nutrients for the strenuous day ahead.

"Are you coming back here?" Melissa asked.

"What do you mean?" Natalie frowned.

"I mean when you finally follow the path over the mountain, will you come back here? You guys seem to have accumulated a lot of stuff. I was just wondering what was going to happen to your house and all of your things?" Melissa looked from woman to woman. Clearly this thought had not crossed their minds before now.

"We don't know what's on the other side," Lola said quietly. "We don't know if we'll want to come back, but I guess it's nice to know we could if we wanted to."

"And now the house is here when someone else comes along the path," Natalie nodded. "I hope that we don't need all of this equipment where we are going. I don't see another mountain in the distance. Once we're over, I expect it'll be a lot easier."

They spent the evening packing their bags and doing some last minute research and agreed to have an early night. Melissa had slept well up until now, but tonight she lay awake for a long time. All of this preparation had made her more apprehensive instead of more confident. Anxious to get on her way but very scared of the path ahead, she tossed and turned for a long time. Part of her wanted desperately to get on with her journey, but the other part was really frightened to leave this house.

Not having slept particularly well, she was up and ready by the time the others had arranged to get up. At the allocated departure time, she opened the door to the room she had been using, expecting to see the others ready to go, but was surprised to find them both still in their pyjamas. Natalie was pacing back and forth, and Lola was sitting on the couch with book open on her lap. They were both clearly upset.

"We're not going today," Natalie exploded when she saw Melissa.

"Why? What's wrong?" Melissa asked, sitting on the couch beside Lola. Lola, who was usually so nervous, had an aura of calm about her this morning. Looking up from the book she was reading, she smiled confidently at Melissa.

"I got up early because I realized that we hadn't checked the Almanac to make sure it was an auspicious day to be travelling. I looked up today, and it's not really a very good day to travel. Just to make sure, I looked up each of our Chinese Horoscopes and checked our individual signs against a different Almanac and discovered that Natalie really shouldn't be going anywhere today."

"So we aren't leaving today. Unpack your bag. Let's have some breakfast!" Natalie threw her hands in the air with each sentence she spat out and was still pacing furiously.

"Well, if we aren't leaving today, when are we leaving?" Melissa wondered.

"Well, after I checked today I did some cross-referencing again for the rest of the month. It turns out that the next day that we could all safely travel is 10 days from now," Lola said, motioning to the calendar in front of her now turned to a different page. The kittens on this page were peeking out of a paper bag. There was a new red circle around the box for the eighth of the month.

"Ten days!" Natalie stormed back to her room and slammed the door. They could hear her swearing to herself as she took her energy out on her closet and cupboard doors. Soon she came back into the room dressed in her grey tracksuit.

"I'll see you for breakfast," she spat as she left the house. They could hear her footsteps as she ran away into the forest.

"Don't worry about her," Lola said. "She always gets like this. She'll be better when she gets back and we get back to planning. She's just disappointed." Lola headed into the kitchen to make breakfast. Melissa could hear her humming as she rummaged in the cupboards.

Picking up the book that Lola had showed her, Melissa looked for today's date. Sure enough, it clearly showed that travel was not suggested. Secretly glad, she propped her feet up on the coffee table, accidentally knocking the calendar onto the floor. As she bent to retrieve it, she saw that it had opened to another month. There were black x's and a red circle on it. Sitting back with the calendar on her lap, she leafed through the pages. As far back as the calendar went, on every month there was at least one, and sometimes two or three red circles around a date. There were black x's through the rest of the days. Melissa quickly counted them up. They had intended to leave fifteen times before today during the last five months alone.

"What would you like for breakfast?" Lola asked, poking her head around the door. "I think we'll be able to have something a bit wicked today. I was thinking pancakes!"

"Sure, that would be great," Melissa said, getting up and taking the calendar with her to hang on the door again. "Lola, how many times have you intended to leave before today?"

"Oh, I don't know. I've lost count now," Lola answered, stretching up on her toes to reach the flour. "We keep making deadlines, but they're flexible. We just haven't been ready. I think we might have been ready today though. It's a shame we didn't check that Almanac a few weeks ago when we set the new deadline. Never mind. We'll be really ready the next time. Next time we'll do it!" She moved about the kitchen in her bare feet and pyjamas, frying sausages and making pancakes with a cool efficiency. By the time they heard Natalie coming back inside, there was a stack of golden pancakes, a plate of sausages, and a bowl of fruit salad on the table.

"Looks great," Natalie said, wiping her forehead with a towel. "Just let me get cleaned up, and I'll be with you."

Lola was just pouring the maple syrup when Natalie joined them, fluffing her wet hair with another towel. Sitting down, she piled her plate high with pancakes.

"Where did you run today?" Lola asked, passing her the syrup.

"Back up the path, same as usual," Natalie chirped. Her anger had disappeared. "Back at it after breakfast then. We have ten more days to get ready!" Melissa looked at them both and shook her head a little.

"Doesn't it bother you how many deadlines you've set and changed?" She asked Natalie.

"It did at first," Natalie nodded, her mouth full of pancake. "But then we just set a new deadline and start again. We weren't ready. We'll start the countdown again today.

So the training began again. They meditated, they walked, they ran, and they researched. What Melissa didn't know about wildflowers that grew on a mountain hadn't been written. They spent so much time on the path leading to the house that Melissa thought she could probably do it blindfolded. The closer they got to their deadline, the more nervous Melissa got. What if they got there and discovered that they weren't ready? More importantly, what if they started off and then failed?

She wasn't terribly upset ten days later when they woke up to rain and had to postpone the journey. She was even less upset three weeks after that when Lola woke up with a cold and they had to postpone again. They would leave eventually. Every time they set a new deadline she happily unpacked her bag and got back to getting ready. The mountain wasn't going anywhere. They'd get to it when they were ready.

It was a sunny Thursday afternoon, three days before their latest deadline, when a whiff of change arrived in the clearing. Lola was inside reading up on edible mountain plants, Natalie was getting changed after her run, and Melissa was outside on the porch going through the contents of their first aid kits when she looked up to see a stranger coming towards her.

"Hello!" Melissa called out warmly, putting down a roll of bandages and standing up.

"Hi there," the woman said, stepping onto the porch.

"I'm Melissa," Melissa smiled, stepping forward to shake the woman's hand.

"Charlotte," the woman smiled warmly. "Do you live here?" She asked, looking around her. Melissa thought back to her own first impressions of the house, remembering how odd it had looked in the middle of the forest. Charlotte took a dusty bag from her back and put it on the step.

"Not really," Melissa said. "I'm just staying here for a little while before I continue on over the mountain."

"Oh," Charlotte nodded, her smile fading. "Are there many people here?"

"Three," Melissa answered, calling Natalie and Lola to come and meet their guest.

"Hello!" Natalie beamed as she stepped onto the porch. "I'm Natalie."

"Natalie, Lola, this is Charlotte," Melissa stepped in quickly, trying to remember her manners. She hadn't needed them in a long time.

"I'm very pleased to meet you," Lola said, loitering just inside the door. "You must be very thirsty, would you like a drink?"

"Yes, please," Charlotte smiled, turning around to take in the clearing. "Isn't this beautiful!" It was more of a comment than a question. "How long have you been here?" Charlotte asked, sitting down on the porch step.

"I've been here for just over six years," Natalie answered. "Lola's been nearly three years, and Melissa has been with us for about three months." Natalie smiled at Melissa, who looked back at her in amazement. Had it really been three months already? She sat down on the porch step next to Charlotte, her head buzzing. She felt sick.

"Wow, that's a long time," Charlotte said. "And what do you do?"

"We're in training," Natalie answered.

"For what?" Charlotte asked. Lola appeared at the door, pushing it open with the tray she held in her hands.

"To climb the mountain," Melissa answered dully. Accepting her glass from Lola, she held it in both hands.

"Oh," Charlotte said, looking a bit puzzled. "And when are you going to climb the mountain?"

"We're leaving in three days!" Natalie said brightly, taking a big gulp of her lemonade. Melissa looked at her glass, remembering the first glass of lemonade she had sipped in this house three long months ago. She couldn't bring herself to drink it now. Her throat felt tight and sore. The others were chatting beside her, but she couldn't hear them, and the lemonade was sour on her tongue even though she hadn't had any.

"Well, thank you very much for the drink," Charlotte said, getting up and dusting herself off. "I should be going." Melissa stared up at her, realizing what was happening.

"Oh don't go," Lola smiled, putting the empty glasses back on the tray. "Stay the night. You won't get very far before it gets dark. Better yet, you could stay and leave with us in a couple of days. We could use the help."

"Thank you, that is a very kind offer," Charlotte smiled. "But I think I know which direction I need to go in. If I follow my path, I should be all right. I'd really like to keep moving now that I have started."

"Really?" Natalie looked at her nervously. "We can't convince you to stay? It's quite a big mountain, and you aren't carrying very much gear."

"I'm sure that I have everything I need," Charlotte smiled, picking up her bag and slinging it over her shoulder. "Thank you again for the drink." She stepped off the porch and started up the path beside the house. Just before she was out of sight, she turned and waved. Dazed, they all waved back.

The three women remained on the porch for a few minutes after Charlotte disappeared, then Lola got up and took the tray back into the house. Natalie followed her inside, but Melissa sat by herself on the step for a long time watching the path that led towards the mountain. It didn't change, and Charlotte didn't come back.

Dinner was unusually subdued as they were each lost in their own thoughts, and they went to bed earlier than usual. For the next two days, they worked harder than they had before. On the last night, they packed their bags, ready for an early morning start. Before she went to bed, Melissa sat on the porch again to stare at the path. It frustrated her that she could only see a short distance in either direction. She knew where it came from, but Charlotte had appeared on that path, so she didn't know all of its secrets. She knew where it led, but only because she could see the top of the mountain in the distance. Hoping for an answer, she watched the path until it got too dark to see, but it wouldn't show her anything.

It was still dark when Melissa woke up to the sound of arguing. Still in her pyjamas, she stumbled into the living room to see what was going on. Someone had left the kitchen window open the evening before, and an animal had climbed in and eaten most of the food that they had packed for the journey. Lola and Natalie were locked in an argument over which one of them had left the window open.

"Sorry to wake you Melissa," Natalie grumbled. "You might as well go back to bed, we aren't going anywhere today." She turned back to Lola and started arguing again. Melissa nodded even though they weren't paying attention to her and went back to her bedroom. Although she was sleepy, she couldn't get back to sleep. They were extending the deadline again. They were changing the rules again. They were staying where they were again. Why was she having trouble remembering her life? Why wasn't she in a hurry to get back to it? What was she so afraid of? Why hadn't Charlotte been afraid? Melissa climbed out of bed and took a blanket with her onto the porch, wanting to watch the path again. Surely Charlotte would come back.

"I'm scared of you," she whispered to the mountain. Pulling the blanket more tightly around her, she watched the path and waited for a reply. She didn't know what she expected, but she watched anyway. Around her, the morning began gently. The birds began to sing, and the sun peeked over the treetops. The colours around her got brighter and brighter, and still she sat, feeling more stuck than ever.

"Melissa, are you coming in for breakfast?" Lola asked, leaning around the door. Melissa could only answer with a shake of her head. A few minutes later Lola brought out a mug of tea and a piece of toast on a plate. Melissa sat and watched the whole morning go by. Natalie went and came back from a run, watching Melissa nervously as she climbed the stairs. At lunchtime, Melissa got up and the others hoped that she would come inside. Instead, she stretched, walked up the path towards the edge of the clearing, stopped, looked into the forest for a few minutes and then turned around and walked back to her blanket and her step.

"Melissa, would you like to come in and have some tea?" Natalie called cheerfully through the open door. For the first time all day, Melissa perked up. With a deep breath, she stretched her shoulders up towards her ears and exhaled loudly. Carrying her blanket, she finally got up and went inside the house. Instead of sitting down for tea, however, she went into her bedroom, got dressed, made the bed, and picked up the bag that had been packed and unpacked so many times. She knew she was ready. It didn't make what she was about to do less scary, but at least she knew she had done all she could. Settling the straps securely over her shoulders, she walked into the kitchen.

"Natalie, Lola, thank you very much for all that you have done for me. Thank you for your kind hospitality. Thank you for letting me stay here, but I am afraid I have to go now," she said firmly.

"No!" Lola cried. "Oh, Melissa, wait and come with us. We'll leave as soon as we get some more food packed."

"Thank you for the kind offer, but I need to go now," Melissa said, reaching forward to shake Natalie's hand. Natalie had gone very quiet. Lola darted out of the kitchen and came back with a box of matches.

"Here, take these," Lola smiled, holding the matches towards Melissa. "You might need them."

"Thank you Lola," Melissa smiled, tucking the box into her knapsack. "I think I already have everything else I need."

"Are you sure you wouldn't like some lemonade or something to eat first?" Lola asked, fluttering around the kitchen, looking for something else to give her.

"No, thank you," Melissa said again. Natalie stared at her in anger. Without saying a word, Natalie turned and left the room, slamming the door behind her. Melissa looked at Lola again.

"When she comes back, tell her I said thank you and that I hope to see you both again someday. And tell her I had to go." With those words, Melissa turned and walked out of the house.

Stepping down from the porch, she allowed herself one last look back down the path that she knew well enough to walk it with her eyes closed. She had gone back and forth that way for so long that, for a moment, she had doubts about her ability to leave it. With a deep breath, she turned her body to face the other direction. Taking one step and then another and then another, she was soon at the edge of the clearing. Without pausing or looking back, she bent a little to avoid the low hanging branches and entered the forest.

Chapter Six

I t was a long time before she was able to breathe properly again. The momentum of beginning and the braveness of leaving the others behind carried her deep into the forest. She felt tough and strong. Shoulders down and head up, she strode further and further away from the cabin in the woods. When she had been walking for a little while, she began to think about where the last three months had gone. She still couldn't believe that it had been so long.

Deep in her thoughts, she tripped over another root. This time she had been going so quickly that she stumbled forward and fell to the ground. Winded, she rolled over into a sitting position to assess the damage. Brushing pine needles and dirt from her hands and knees, she looked around her. Trees hid the mountain from her, but she could see the path that was ahead. She hadn't properly looked at it before now. It was well worn in places, but in others it was terribly overgrown. It didn't make sense that parts of it were smooth and easy while others were such hard work. Wouldn't the same path be worn in the same way?

"How much further do I need to go today?" She asked the trees. "Will there be a dry place for me to sleep tonight?" They didn't answer. "I've never slept outside on my own before," she mused out loud. Her voice sounded strange as it hung in the air. She didn't know who she was talking to, but it made her feel better to say it out loud. No part of her wanted to keep walking, but she forced herself to get up. Sitting here wasn't going to get her anywhere. The last time she had kept going she had found something interesting. Perhaps today would work out the same way. It might look like nothing but forest, but she was sure that there were more secrets to be found.

Focusing on each small step, Melissa followed her path. She would pause periodically to get food or water out of her bag and ask the trees a few questions, but generally she kept moving. No longer overwhelmed by the weirdness of her situation, she was beginning to feel frustrated by her own lack of control. Once when she was little, she remembered she had looked down at an anthill and then up into the sky and wondered who was staring down at her. She had often wondered if life was just some big science experiment where you were under a bright light in the daytime so that you could be studied and the night time stars were just holes punched in the top of a box so that you could breathe. Feeling just like that now, she pinched herself again for good measure.

Melissa was bored of herself. In an attempt to focus on something different, she began mentally walking through her apartment. Moving through each room, she tried to remember what things had looked like the morning she left. It frustrated her that she couldn't remember if she'd done the dishes or not. She hoped that whoever had packed her bag had cleaned up her kitchen.

Finished with her apartment, she decided to take a tour of her childhood home. Starting at the front door, she visualized going inside and moving through the different rooms. The kitchen had been the first room you entered, so she paused there until she had remembered every detail from the colour of the pink and green flowered wallpaper to the placement of the mugs on the windowsill above the sink. She remembered where the phone had sat and how one of the chairs around the table had held her mother's handmade red cushion. When she had toured the kitchen, she went around all of the other rooms. It eventually occurred to her that no one was home.

"Hello," she called as she stood at the bottom of the stairs looking up.

"Hello there!"

Melissa jumped and let out a shriek. The voice had not come from her house, but right beside her.

"I'm sorry. I didn't mean to frighten you, but you said hello first," a woman said, clearly confused. Melissa had stopped walking and was now trying to catch her breath and get her heart beating normally again.

"No, that's okay," Melissa explained. "I was just somewhere else." The woman lifted her eyebrows in confusion, but she smiled with one corner of her mouth and stuck out her hand.

"I'm Emma," she said. Melissa reached forward and shook her hand warmly. They both laughed at how strange it was to be shaking hands in the woods.

"I'm Melissa."

"Well Melissa, it's nice to meet you. We heard you coming and wanted to catch you and see if you wanted to join us tonight," Emma gestured a little way off the path to Melissa's right.

"Who's we?" Melissa asked.

"Me and Grace," Emma answered. "Follow me." They had only gone a few steps when they came to another path through the woods and another woman squatting down beside a small fire.

"This one is my path," Emma smiled. "And this is Grace. We met a couple of days ago when our paths nearly ran into each other. We've been walking side by side ever since. Oh, it's been so nice to have someone to talk to! When we heard you coming, we hoped that your path would join ours too." Grace stood up and came forward to shake Melissa's hand, brushing herself off as she moved. They offered Melissa a log to sit on and she sat quietly for a moment as she took in her surroundings.

She could see what Emma had meant about their paths. Just a few feet from where they sat, two paths went by, side-by-side. She was glad that they had called out to her. How incredible that she could have walked right by them and not noticed. She wondered if she had passed that closely to anyone else today. It made her shiver.

"Are you cold?" Emma asked. Melissa nodded. Now she had stopped moving, she was indeed cold and a little bit nervous. Opening her bag she found her grey sweater and pulled it on, using the distraction to study the two women. They were of a similar age to her and both were wearing walking shoes, but that's where the similarity ended. Emma was short and thin and had long blonde hair tied in two long pigtails just below her ears. Warm green eyes radiated friendliness but also a deep sadness. Melissa thought that she even looked a little bit sad when she was laughing, which was most of the time. Grace was a little bit taller with dark olive skin and dark brown hair that she wore loosely gathered into a knot. She was as curvy as Emma was thin. They couldn't have been more different physically, but Grace held a similar look in her eyes. Melissa wondered if her eyes looked the same.

"How long have you been travelling?" Grace asked.

"You know, I seem to have lost all track of time," Melissa answered honestly, rummaging in her bag for a bottle of water. Finding one, she drank deeply.

"Oh, me too, me too!" Emma exclaimed. "I realized yesterday that I have been gone for five months. FIVE! I would like to talk to someone in charge, because I can't leave my life for that long."

"I know," Grace squealed, "I have a company to run. I don't know what they are doing without me there!"

"Did you guys start at Selene's house?" Melissa asked. Both women shook their heads.

"No, I started in an office with a woman named Bonnie," Grace said. "I don't remember much about it. I left pretty late at night and ended up staying in a barn with a bunch of hippies for the first few weeks."

"Hippies?" Melissa giggled.

"So what do you guys think is going on?" Emma asked, poking the fire with a stick, not wanting to look either of them in the eye. "Do you think that this is real?"

"It can't be!" Grace whispered. "I have been trying to wake myself up for months. I wonder if maybe I've been in an accident and I am actually unconscious in a hospital."

"So we are figments of your imagination?" Emma laughed.

"Maybe," Grace answered.

"I've been pinching myself trying to wake up," Melissa admitted. "But I've never had such a long dream before."

"I feel a bit like Dorothy in the *Wizard of Oz*," Emma laughed again. "Only that makes you two the scarecrow and the tin man!"

"No brains and no heart?" Grace smiled. "I wonder where we'll meet no courage."

"No, I think that one is me!" Melissa laughed. They were all quiet for a minute and then Emma started poking the fire again.

"So if we aren't dreaming and we aren't in a collective coma, are we dead?"

"If this is heaven, I need to get back and tell Oprah," Grace joked. "'Cause this is nothing like I thought!" They all laughed again.

"So then where are we?" Emma had stopped laughing.

"I don't know," Melissa answered quietly. "It's all been so strange. Things and people have disappeared, food appears in my bag when I need it, three months just went by in what felt like days. I can't get my head around all of it. I think I am going to have to pretend that this is all a dream."

"Maybe it's a collective one. Maybe we are in each other's dreams," Grace said. "I like that better than being in some sort of purgatory or coma."

"If we ever find someone in charge, we'll ask them," Melissa smiled. "I wish I could ask that Anna a thing or two right now!" She started rummaging in her bag. Feeling hungry, she pulled out a banana. Curling her lip in distaste, she put it down beside her and started rummaging again. Out came a turkey sandwich. Shrugging, she unwrapped it. She had wanted something warm and cozy, but she doubted that she'd find hot macaroni and cheese in there with her clothes and shoes. Emma and Grace were both digging into their bags for something to eat.

"Can I have that banana if you aren't going to eat it?" Grace asked. Melissa nodded and handed it over, her mouth too full to answer.

"So where do you think you'll go next?" Emma asked, her mouth full of roast beef wrap.

"Oh, goodness knows," Melissa said, finishing her sandwich and wiping a smear of mayonnaise from the corner of her mouth. Not quite satisfied, she pulled her bag towards her again and realized that it was warm to the touch. Intrigued, she opened it. On top of her clothes was a square plastic container with a purple lid. Lifting the container out of her bag, Melissa shook her head in disbelief. There in front of her was a portion of her mother's homemade macaroni and cheese. And it was still hot.

None of the women had ever expected that a portion of macaroni and cheese would freak them out as much as that one did. Melissa placed it on a rock by the fire, and they all sat and looked at it for a long time. They had all had food and drink out of their bags before now, but never something that they had specifically thought of. Afraid that it might actually taste of homemade macaroni and cheese, Melissa didn't want to eat it. Finally, Emma was brave enough to ask what they were all thinking.

"Where are we?" She whispered.

There was no answer.

When they packed up in the morning, they left the macaroni and cheese sitting where Melissa had left it the night before. They chatted about the weather and about the hard ground and about the fact that there had been no insects bothering them while they slept. They didn't talk about where they were going to go next, and they didn't stop for any breakfast, even though their stomachs were rumbling. When they were packed and loaded, they each stood quietly back on her own path.

"If we go in different directions today, it was very nice to meet you," Melissa called. Emma giggled, and Grace waved her hand.

"I hope that we stay together today! It's nice to have the company," Grace said.

With a final glance at their campsite, they started walking. Melissa listened to Grace and Emma talking and wondered if she would be alone again by evening.

"Well, look who's here!" Emma smiled as Melissa's path veered directly beside hers. "Looks like you get to walk with us for a little while!"

They walked for a few hours, chatting about what they said were their 'real lives.' Lunchtime came and went and they didn't stop. They were determined not to talk about food. The macaroni had caused food to become a symbol of their confusion. By not eating, they could pretend that everything was normal. It was late afternoon when Grace suddenly stopped in the middle of the path. The others walked on a few steps and then looked back for her. She was cocking her head to the side.

"Listen, do you hear that?" She asked, craning her neck to the side. "Do you hear that kind of roaring sound?" The others stopped and lifted their noses in the air, squinting their eyes as they listened. Sure enough, they could hear a noise. Melissa thought it sounded like a concert without the music or the ocean during a storm.

"What is that?" Emma asked, shaking her head.

"I don't know. Does it sound friendly? It's a strange noise." Melissa whispered.

Another hour went by and with each passing minute and each passing step the sound grew louder and louder. Melissa's stomach growled. The sound in her stomach sounded eerily similar to the sound she could hear all around her.

"Look, I think the trees stop up there," Emma whispered, pointing ahead of them on the path. Sure enough, they could see light through the trees in a way they hadn't all day. The edge of the forest was coming. The roar was almost on top of them now. Grasping hands for courage, they walked out of the woods.

Chapter Seven

The roar came to life as a seven story, round building. Sliding doors on every floor gave access to four balconies that swept in swirls around the building. The roar rumbled from the building's belly, and the women realized that it was actually made up of hundreds of voices, all raised in conversation.

As they walked closer, Melissa could see that many, many paths led in this direction. There were so many that the ground outside had been walked bare. Melissa studied the path at her feet carefully. It would be so easy to forget which one was hers with so many going off in so many different directions. Her path had travelled right by the little cottage in the woods, but instead of following it, she had gone inside and it had been three months before she had started moving again. It was no surprise to her, however, when the path led right up to the front door: she had to go inside.

Nearly two stories high and created from dark brown wood, the door that stood before them did not look friendly. Once it had been intricately carved, but over the years, many hands had worn the images away and now its surface was blurry and a little grotesque. Grace was the only one brave enough to knock.

"Do you have a reservation?" Instead of the big wooden door opening, a woman appeared beside them. Her bleached-blonde hair was piled up on the top of her head in a beehive, and she wore a tight lime green pencil-skirt and matching jacket, a telephone operator's headset, and dark green horn-rimmed glasses. Busy staring at her, none of them thought to answer. Rolling her eyes, she adjusted her glasses, pursed her heavily lipsticked lips and waited for a moment. Tapping her foot in irritation, she tried again in a clipped, nasal tone. "Do you have a reservation?"

"I don't think so," Emma stammered. "Do we need one?" The woman rolled her eyes again and snapped her fingers. A large book appeared in her hands. Holding it in one hand, she ran a red-lacquered fingernail along the page. Muttering to herself, she turned a few pages forward and then backwards.

"I think I might be able to fit you in. Let me just check." Pushing a button on her headset, she spoke loudly and nasally into the microphone. "Yah, Shelley? Yah, I have a party of three here ready to start. Yah. Yah. Can I let them through then? Yah. Okay." Taking a pen from where it had been stuck in her knot of hair, she looked up at them expectantly. "Name?"

"Um, Grace," Grace started.

"That's enough," the woman interrupted. "I actually don't care who you are. You're all the same in here really. Go through the door, take the steps to the second level and wait for Shelley. She'll show you to your seats." With another snap of her fingers, the door yawned open slowly. Melissa took one last look up before she went inside. Just above where she stood there was a woman looking over the balcony. Melissa smiled, but the woman just shook her head and turned away.

Inside it was dark and cool. The room that they had entered had a black and white chequered floor and three closed doors in the wall directly ahead of them. There was no indication of which one hid the stairs.

"Oh, can you smell that? Emma wrinkled her nose as she sniffed the air. "They're eating roast chicken!"

"That's not what I smell," Grace whispered. "I think that they must be having something else. I can smell onions and garlic." Melissa sniffed too, but she was certain that they must be on the dessert course because she could smell sweet, fresh whipped cream.

"So which door?" Grace whispered again.

"Grace, I hardly think you have to whisper," Emma giggled. "No one behind these doors is paying any attention to us!" Grace smiled timidly but remained quiet. Melissa looked around her again and sniffed the air. The smells and sounds of people eating were not contained behind the three doors. It felt instead as if a ghostly meal was swirling around them. Gentle at first, the longer she stood there, the more aggressive it felt. Needing to move, Melissa tried the closest door. Smiling widely, she stepped back and revealed the staircase to the others. It looked more like a fire escape than anything else, but it meant that they could get out of the lobby.

"I don't know about you, but I am starving!" Emma exclaimed, pushing past Melissa through the open door. They climbed the stairs quickly, their steps echoing between the metal steps and the light green walls. When they reached a landing they stopped, nervous about going through the next door. None of them wanted to speak, and they hesitated for a moment longer. Finally, Grace reached out to open the door. She had barely touched the handle when the door flew open.

"Where have you been?" A screechy voice greeted them. The voice and the noise and the heat and the scent and the energy that swirled through the open door assaulted them, and they all took a step back.

"Come in," the woman smiled, realizing that they weren't going to move. "I have just the table for you! I'm Shelley. Follow me please." Shelley was tall and had a bleached blonde hairdo much like the woman who had met them downstairs. When she looked at them, it was over the rim of a pair of glasses that were perched on the end of her nose.

"Now, I have a lovely seat by the window for you," she was saying as she walked, her voice thick with years of smoke. "They don't come up very often, but the last woman there left this morning. When I heard that there were three of you, I knew I'd have to give you the seat by the window." As she said this, she waved at a small dark haired woman in an apron who followed them with an armload of menus.

The room was crowded with tables and had a high, vaulted ceiling. The combination of very dark and very lightly coloured wood gave the impression of an enormous ski chalet. The front of the room swept around in a large arc, with windows running the full length. A buffet had been placed along the back wall, opposite the windows.

"Here we are," Shelley exclaimed brightly. She stood and waited for them to sit down and then she put her hand on the shoulder of the woman holding the menus. "Now, this is Hannah and she will be your waitress for most of the time you are here. If you need anything, just ask her." With a nod, Shelley was off, threading her way through the tables. Hannah didn't watch her go. Instead, she smiled and handed out the menus.

"Well, as Shelley said, I will be your waitress. If you need anything, all you have to do is ask. There are several options available to you. We have a menu, which you will see is quite extensive, but we also have a buffet along the back wall, and if you look there to your right you will see that there is a door through there. Behind that door, you will find a fully stocked kitchen ready for your use. You may have anything that you find in the cupboards, fridge or freezer, it's all included. If you want to eat something from the buffet, all you have to do is go up there and get it. If you want something from the menu, all you have to do is say it out loud and it will be brought to you. Don't worry about plates and cutlery; we will take care of those too. Any questions?" Without giving them time to answer, she ploughed on. "Great. Well, I will leave you to look at your menus. Have a little explore if you like, and I will come back soon." With that, Hannah turned on her heel and walked in the direction of the buffet.

"Is she kidding?" Grace whispered. "I don't get it."

"I'm so hungry," Emma said hunching over and holding onto her stomach. "I can't take it! All of these smells are making my stomach growl. I wonder if we are going to get some bread to nibble on." Barely a moment later, Hannah appeared, carrying a basket full of bread. With a smile, she was gone again, leaving the steaming fragrant basket behind.

"Okay, will someone please tell me what is going on?" Grace whispered again. There was real panic in her voice and her cheeks were becoming flushed.

"I think we are supposed to eat," Melissa shrugged. "I'm not sure. I am going to go and have a look around, does anyone want to come?" Grace shook her head miserably, and Emma reached for a soft, white roll so Melissa got up and left them behind, deciding to start with the buffet. As she watched, one woman walked straight up to the buffet, put something on her plate and walked away. Another woman was hovering with an empty plate in her hand as if hoping someone else could make the decision for her.

"Have you been here very long?" Melissa asked. The woman nodded unhappily and walked away. Melissa watched her go and then turned her attention back to the banquet in front of her. At one end of the buffet, huge pots full of soups and stews and casseroles merrily steamed up the stack of glasses beside them.

Roasts of meat with all of the trimmings, a hundred different kinds of salad, loaves and loaves of bread, sandwich fillings, vegetables and sauces were presented beside each other with no apparent order. In fact, the only order Melissa could see on the buffet was that an entire section of it was completely dedicated to chocolate. Brownies, squares, and huge chunks of fudge were balanced beside tubs of chocolate ice cream and vats of warm chocolate sauce. Delicate chocolate tarts, profiteroles, and cheesecake shared platters with exquisitely hand painted chocolates. Even though she was closer to the salads when she noticed that part of the buffet, the smell of chocolate beckoned her, and Melissa was drawn in. All she wanted in that whole moment was a cookie, but she resisted.

Feeling a little faint, Melissa turned away from the buffet and went towards the shared kitchen. As she opened the door and peeked in, she heard a shuffling. A women with a guilty look on her face was in the process of shutting one cupboard doors. Still chewing, and brushing crumbs from the corner of her mouth, she hurried past Melissa and back into the dining room.

Set up like a home kitchen, the room came complete with a stove, a sink and a refrigerator. Pots and pans, plates, cutlery and drinking glasses filled the shelves above the sink. Melissa opened a few cupboards and found them very well stocked. Peanut butter, Marmite, marmalade, and seven types of jam nestled beside jars of lemon curd and chocolate hazelnut spread. Bags of cookies and packages of crackers provided lots of delicious crunchy layers to work with. Cooking sauces and tins of soup, oils and vinegars, and other cooking and baking supplies rounded out the cupboards. Opening the fridge, she saw that it too was well stocked. In fact, Melissa couldn't think of a thing that she would ever want to eat that wasn't there.

Running her finger along the top of the counter, Melissa wandered down to the other end of the room. Here, the kitchen opened out into a kind of greenhouse. There were no windows in the room, but there were rows and rows of plants, all growing under bright lights. As Melissa watched, a buzzer went off and a watering system switched on. Herbs and vegetables shuddered under the fake rain. A few minutes later the alarm sounded again, and the water switched off. Melissa wasn't sure she liked watching plants on life support.

"So what did you find?" Grace asked as Melissa returned to the table. As Melissa told them what she had found, Emma buttered a piece of thick brown bread and Grace sat with her hands in her lap looking sad. Brightening a little at the mention of the kitchen, Grace was soon squirming in her seat as the others looked at their menus.

The menu was thirty-seven pages long. Anything Melissa had ever eaten in her life was there. She was overwhelmed with choice.

"What are you going to have?" Emma asked. Melissa remembered the cookie, but she decided that that would be irresponsible.

"I think I am going to go up to the buffet and have one of their salads," Melissa said, closing her menu and putting it back down on the table. "I can't look at this menu anymore. It's just too much! Do either of you want to come with me?"

"No thanks," Emma said, "I think I am going to order from the menu."

"I'll come," Grace murmured, putting her own menu on top of Melissa's. Chilled and heated plates sat in separate piles at one end of the buffet, so they started there.

"I can't believe how much there is to choose from," Grace whispered. "What are you going to have?"

"I think I am going to have some salad," Melissa answered, choosing a chilled plate. "I'm going to try to be good. What about you?"

"Oh me too," Grace said. "There's too much to choose from." They filled their plates with lettuce leaves, shredded carrot, tomatoes, and cucumber. Melissa smiled when she saw the little pots of dressing and croutons and bacon, remembering those from restaurants she had gone to when she was little. Choosing a nice oily-vinegary dressing, she self-consciously added croutons and bits of bacon, feeling a bit childish. They stuck to the dressing just like she remembered. Grace left off the bacon bits. Arriving back at their table, they were just in time to see Emma taking her first bite of a big, juicy hamburger. Melissa's stomach rumbled at the sight.

"Diet starts tomorrow!" Emma laughed, her mouth full of food. Sighing with pleasure, she settled back into her chair and chewed slowly. As they ate, they chatted some more about their lives. Melissa could feel her shoulders relax for the first time in a long time. This, finally, felt real. This felt like they were just three new friends out for dinner who were eating ordinary food in an ordinary restaurant. She hadn't pinched herself for at least an hour.

"I think I am just going to have a look at what else is up there," Melissa announced. Her salad was finished, but she wanted more. Emma was just finishing her hamburger, and Grace was still pushing lettuce around on her plate. Neither of them wanted to move yet, so Melissa got up and went back to the buffet by herself. Ignoring the dessert section, she walked over to the hot food, feeling like she needed something warm and comforting. Eyeing a fresh batch of mashed potatoes, she smiled. That was more like it! Soon her plate was piled high with mashed potatoes covered with rich, thick gravy. She felt decadent and excited and dismayed all at the same time.

"I'll only eat a little of it," she murmured to herself. Her conscience poked at her, but she ignored it. Back at her table she found Emma starting on a huge slice of chocolate cake.

"You only live once!" Emma grinned, her teeth full of chocolate. Melissa smiled back at her, admiring Emma's exuberance. Grace was still playing with her salad.

"Aren't you going to have anything else?" Melissa asked.

"No," Grace smiled, putting her fork down. "I'm actually pretty full."

"Oh, I wish I could listen to my stomach like that," Melissa said, sprinkling salt on her food. "But I just can't stop once I've started!" Grace just smiled and toyed with the edge of her plate.

When their plates were clear again, Hannah asked them if they would like to be shown to their room. It was only then that they realized that they hadn't even thought about what was next. Their bags had been sitting against the window waiting for them, so they picked them up and followed Hannah up another set of stairs.

"If you need or want anything, the dining room is never closed or locked," Hannah said, pushing through a door at the top of the steps and into a corridor lined with doors. The carpet was so thick under their feet, they couldn't hear their own steps. Hannah paused in front of room 37 and turned the knob.

"Here is your room. Breakfast is whenever you get there tomorrow. Sleep well," Hannah said as she turned and moved to go.

"Wait," Grace called. "We don't have a key to the door."

"Don't worry," Hannah smiled gently and kept walking. "You won't need one. We don't have any problems here. Good night."

Comfortable and simple, the room held three beds, three bedside tables, and a single armchair. Towels and linens and robes were soft and white, there were new, soft pyjamas on the beds, and the trio squealed when they saw that there were also three bathrooms, each with its own shower and brand new toothbrush waiting for them. It was not long before they were all clean, dried, and tucked up tightly in bed.

The only markers of time were the showers she had in the morning. Meals and naps blurred together until the days became hazy. They weren't sure when they would be leaving or what they were supposed to be doing, and at first they simply didn't care. Emma kept smiling at them, her teeth full of food, and making comments about her diet starting tomorrow. Grace remained subdued. Choosing whatever was the healthiest option, she would eat one small portion of it and then stop eating. Grace's eating habits made Melissa squirm with guilt whenever she noticed. Melissa would start by eating something healthy but would soon find herself on her third, much less healthy course. She knew she should stop, but her hunger just grew bigger with each mouthful.

Something woke her. Melissa lay in bed for a few minutes, wondering what time it was and why she was awake. Rubbing her eyes, she began to see the lines of things in the room. She could just make out the shape of Emma in the next bed. When she squinted across the room, however, Grace's bed was empty. Her own bed was comfortable and soft, and Melissa snuggled deeper into it, trying to go back to sleep, but it wouldn't come. Questions began troubling her, and she finally remembered to ask herself what they were doing here. A sickening thought made her sit up straight. They were sleeping in nice clean beds, and eating ridiculous amounts of food. What if they were presented with a bill at the end of all of this? What if they were meant to pay?

Knowing that she was not going to go back to sleep easily she decided to go down and get herself a drink. Sometimes having a sip of something warm helped her sleep. She got up and put on a robe, creeping out of the room on bare toes.

The corridor was empty and still. Moving silently to the stairs, she hurried down them to the dining room. At the bottom of the stairs, she stopped short. Even though it was the middle of the night, the room was nearly full of people. In the day time the roar came from a room full of people talking and eating and wandering around, but as full as it was, tonight the room was nearly silent. Even when there was more than one person at a table, they weren't talking to each other. The only noises were the soft chink of cutlery and the clunk of china against the table. Here and there a chair scraped back as people got up or sat down. Goosebumps came up on Melissa's neck. This was not a place she wanted to stay long.

Only wanting a drink, Melissa decided that the kitchen was her best bet. Rather than walk directly through the dining room, she kept close to the wall and walked all of the way around. The door gave only the softest of swishes as she pushed it. Once inside she noticed that she was not alone. There were no lights on, but Melissa could see that there were several figures sitting in the semi-darkness. None of them looked at her as she passed. One woman sat in front of the open refrigerator eating something out of a bowl. Another woman was standing facing the cupboards. Melissa could see that she was eating peanut butter straight out of the jar. As Melissa watched, she turned around and slid her back down the cupboards until she was sitting on the floor, her knees drawn up to her chest, holding the jar in one listless hand, and a spoon in the other. Melissa looked from the jar to the woman's tearstained face. It was Grace.

Melissa froze. Grace hadn't noticed her so she turned around and hurried quietly to the door, stealing a quick look back as she was shutting the door behind her. In their robes and in the darkness, the women all looked very much alike.

The only place Melissa could think to go was her own table. Bed was no longer an option, all she could see when she closed her eyes were Grace's tears. Come to think of it, she remembered the face of the woman sitting in front of the refrigerator and there had been misery there as well. Melissa sat very still and looked at her own hands, not wanting to look at the people sitting around her.

"Can't sleep?" A voice interrupted her thoughts. Melissa shook her head miserably. A mug of tea was placed in front of her. Melissa instinctively wrapped her hands around its warmth.

"May I sit down?" The woman asked, making Melissa look up. It took her brain a few moments to leave the kitchen and really see who was standing in front of her. The woman was tall and slender and was wearing a long purple robe. A pair of silver glasses perched on the end of her nose. Her hair was long and loose and so dark that Melissa could have sworn that it was purple too. Melissa kept staring and then finally realized that what she thought were robes was probably just a dressing gown.

"I'm Mary," the woman said as she sat down on Emma's chair, not waiting for Melissa to answer.

"Melissa," Melissa replied, with an attempt at a smile.

"Is something wrong Melissa?" Mary asked, adjusting her robe and removing her glasses, letting them hang against her chest on a long, silver chain.

"No," Melissa lied. "I just couldn't sleep."

"Liar," Mary smiled. Melissa looked at her in surprise.

"Perhaps I had better introduce myself a little better," Mary began. "My name is Mary, and I am your hostess here."

"Oh," Melissa's mouth fell open. She put down the mug of tea and nervously tried to shake Mary's hand.

"No, no, don't worry," Mary smiled, gesturing with her hands. "I only said that so that I could tell you that I have been keeping an eye on you since you got here."

"You have?" Melissa asked, taking a sip of her tea. It was perfectly warm and tasted like honey. She sighed.

"I have," Mary smiled, enjoying Melissa's reaction to the tea. "I pay attention to everyone who comes in. It's important that I keep track of what and how they are doing."

"Oh, so that you can charge them the right amount?" Melissa asked.

"Charge?" Mary smiled again. "It's not really about that. Tell me Melissa, why do you look so unhappy?"

"I just saw my friend in the kitchen, and she had been crying." Feeling disloyal to Grace, Melissa looked around to see if anyone else was listening.

"Ah, yes, Grace," Mary said, looking sad too. "I just saw her myself. Did you know that she has come down here every night since you arrived?" Melissa shook her head, her expression sorrowful.

"She always goes into the kitchen," Mary said. "Some nights she is in there for a long time and other nights she goes back upstairs fairly quickly. Was she eating peanut butter?" When Melissa nodded yes, Mary went on. "Then she will be there for a little while yet."

"Do you know what's wrong with her?" Melissa asked, staring deeply into her tea.

"Wrong?" Mary looked puzzled by the question.

"Well, you said that she was here every night and I have just seen her crying. Something must be wrong." Melissa raised her eyes and looked at Mary pleadingly. Mary watched her in return for a few moments.

"That's a good question," Mary nodded. "I suppose there was something wrong in the first place, but now it's not about that anymore."

"What do you mean?" Melissa kept watching her face.

"All of our habits and compulsions start with a good reason," Mary said. "But over the years, the reasons become blurred and all we are left with is the reaction to them."

"I don't understand," Melissa said, sipping her tea again.

"When you look around this room, what do you see?" Mary asked. Melissa held her tea like an anchor with both hands and looked around the room.

"I can see a lot of people sitting at tables. They are either eating or drinking or just sitting there. I noticed before that no one seems to be talking very much."

"What you are seeing is the reaction. For many women, eating or not eating was the reaction to something that made them uncomfortable in their past. Most of these women think that food is their problem. Grace thinks food is her problem," Mary said.

"But it isn't food?" Melissa said, confused and very uncomfortable.

"No. Do you want to know what I see?" Mary looked straight into Melissa's eyes. Melissa had to look away, but she nodded.

"I see hunger."

"Hunger? Well, that's obvious. They are all sitting here eating. They wouldn't be eating if they weren't hungry," Melissa sat up straighter and put her mug down on the table.

"But I do not see hunger for food. I see the kind of hunger that roams like an animal through our bodies. I see women hungering for much more than food. Food is just the way that they feed or don't feed that hunger. I see all of the energy that women are wasting fighting with food."

"I really don't think I understand you," Melissa whispered, nervously playing with the edge of the table.

"Okay, well let me ask you a couple of questions," Mary explained. "The day that you arrived here, instead of looking at the menu first, you had a look around didn't you?" When Melissa nodded, Mary went on. "You looked at the buffet and then you looked at the kitchen. With all of the food that was in front of you, what was it that you really really wanted?"

"A cookie," Melissa answered with no hesitation, realizing that she still hadn't had one.

"And what did you eat instead?" Mary asked.

"A salad," Melissa answered.

"Then what did you eat?" Mary asked. Melissa struggled to remember. She had eaten so much; the details were a bit of a blur. "You had the salad, then you had mashed potatoes and gravy, then you had a piece of bread from Emma's bread basket, and then you went back for a piece of chocolate cake with ice cream. You never had the cookie."

"So?" Melissa squirmed.

"Why did you choose the salad over the cookie?" Mary asked.

"Because salad is better for you," Melissa said miserably, realizing how ridiculous she sounded.

"Better for who?" Mary asked.

"It's better for everyone than a cookie is!" Melissa said indignantly.

"Who says?" Mary asked.

"Now come on," Melissa answered angrily. "You are not going to be able to convince me that eating a cookie is better than eating a salad."

"Okay, let me ask you again," Mary said. "Why did you choose the salad over the cookie?"

"Because cookies are bad and salads are good," Melissa sighed, rolling her eyes.

"Why are cookies bad?" Mary asked.

"Because they are bad for me, and because if I ate just one cookie I would have to eat twenty-seven and then I would feel fat and full and sick and guilty," Melissa answered.

"So what you are saying is that cookies are bad because of how you feel after eating them."

"Um," Melissa paused. "Is that what I said?"

"Yes, that is what you said. You don't want to eat a cookie because they make you feel guilty. Is that a fair statement?" Mary still looked calm.

"I guess so," Melissa answered.

"What if I told you that no food was good or bad? What if I told you that food was just food?" Mary asked.

"I'd say you should come over to my house and watch some television and read a few of my magazines," Melissa laughed bitterly. "I'd say it was more than good and bad. I'd say it was good and evil."

"No," Mary insisted. "Food just is."

"Oh, give me a break," Melissa said, rolling her eyes again.

"If you didn't feel any emotion around a cookie, and you wanted one, you could choose a cookie, eat a cookie, enjoy a cookie, and be satisfied with just one cookie, or even just one bite of one," Mary said, poking her finger into the opposite palm with every point. "But because you feel guilt when you eat a cookie, you don't allow yourself one when you truly want one so the need builds up. You feel virtuous when you resist and then when you finally give in and let yourself have a cookie, your body doesn't trust that you can have another one another time, so it goes into overdrive eating as many as it can get its hands on because it might not get any again. All the while you think to yourself that you shouldn't be eating these, and you will never eat them again once you are finished. Then afterwards you feel full and guilty and sick because you ate more than your body needed and the cookies get the blame and the cycle continues."

"I try to be good most of the time," Melissa whispered through the tears that had begun coursing down her cheeks.

"But that's where you make the mistake," Mary said with a gentle shake of her head. "What you eat does not make you good or bad. You are already a good, loveable person no matter what you put in your mouth. Food is not the problem here. Something happened in your life that made you use food to ease a different sort of hunger, and then food became your enemy. But food isn't the enemy. Food just is," Mary was sitting forward now, trying to look into Melissa's eyes.

"What people have forgotten is that we are creatures, just like any other animal on this planet. That scares us, but it's true. We eat, drink, sleep, have sex, and have babies. We treat our bodies like they are robots, but, in fact, we are animals. Our bodies are primal. They would know what we need to eat and when if we would just relax the leash a little, and if we figured out what we were really hungry for.

"Then why is food such hard work?" Melissa asked. "Why can't we just know what we are hungry for?" Mary watched Melissa for a long time without answering. Melissa began to squirm under her gaze. Finally, Mary sat up a little straighter and smiled gently at Melissa.

"Yes, I think you are ready," Mary said, nodding.

"Ready for what?" Melissa asked.

"Come with me, I want you to see something," Mary said.

Mary led Melissa through the maze of tables and chairs, ending up at what Melissa assumed was the reservations computer. Melissa looked at the screen and saw that it showed a floor plan of the dining room, kitchen and the deck outside. There were tiny figures moving around on the screen.

"Mary, I need you to have a look at this one," Hannah said, looking at Melissa out of the corner of her eye. "I think it's gotten much more serious than we thought."

"Excuse me for a moment, Melissa," Mary said, looking closely at the computer and clicking on one of the moving figures. A woman's face filled half of the screen. On the other half was what appeared to be a bill. Melissa suddenly felt very cold and very sweaty. So they did have to pay for all of this.

"I think you're right," Mary murmured, clicking back to the floor plan and putting her finger against the screen. Fumbling, she took hold of her glasses, perched them on her nose, and peered towards the far left corner of the dining room. Melissa followed Mary's gaze. There were quite a few people sitting and having their breakfast now, so Melissa could not tell who Mary was looking at.

"Have Marge go in," Mary said to Hannah. "I think that we need to follow this one up before we have to send her back." Hannah nodded, typing numbers into the computer.

"Too bad," Mary sighed to herself, shaking her head sadly and turning back to Melissa. Before she could say anything, Melissa jumped in.

"Nobody ever said anything about us paying for all of this," Melissa said defensively. "I didn't pack any money, and I know that..."

"It's not like that," Mary said, cutting Melissa off.

"I don't understand," Melissa said, still on the defensive. "I saw that woman's bill on the computer."

"What you saw was not what she owes in money," Mary said. "We don't deal with any money here."

"Then how do you explain the bill?" Melissa asked. Mary removed the glasses again and let them hang on their silver chain.

"We keep track of what you waste," Mary said.

"What we waste?" Melissa responded loudly. "But you just said…"

"No, no, we don't pay attention to what food you waste," Mary said, shaking her head and gesturing for Melissa to be quiet. "You should already know from our talk before that none of this is actually about food."

"I really don't understand," Melissa whined.

"If you'll calm down for a moment, I will try to explain," Mary said. "I need to tell you this again so that you really understand: none of this is about food. When you arrived outside, did you notice how many paths led to these doors?"

"Yes, there were so many you couldn't even see any grass between them," Melissa answered.

"And how did you feel about that?" Mary asked.

"I was a bit nervous actually," Melissa said. "I was worried that I wouldn't be able to find my own path again when it was all over. I didn't want to get stuck here."

"And now?" Mary asked.

"I'm still worried about getting stuck here," Melissa answered. "There seems to be no lesson to learn. There doesn't seem to be an end to it all."

"Oh, there is an end to it all," Mary said. "But not very many people actually find it. An incredible number of women get sent back home from here and never go any farther."

"Why?"

"Because they never ever get it. Some know that there is a lesson to learn but most are so stuck in their own patterns and their own heads that they never see past their next mouthful. We don't measure the food you waste Melissa," Mary said ominously. "We measure the life you waste."

"The life?" Melissa screwed up her face in confusion, cold shivers taking over her skin.

"I want to show you something," Mary said, pulling the silver chain from around her neck. "Do you see that table over there?" Melissa nodded. "Tell me what you see there."

"Well, I see three women having breakfast," Melissa answered.

"And how do they look?" Mary asked.

"Well, they all look fine. One of them looks a little bit sleepy. They seem to be having a nice conversation because they are all laughing and talking. I don't know. It all seems quite ordinary."

"And how old would you say they were?" Mary continued.

"Oh, I don't know. I'd say one of them was in her twenties, and the other two are somewhere in their mid-thirties. Why?" Melissa turned her attention from the table and back to Mary.

"Well, things are not always as they seem," Mary said cryptically. "What you don't see is how much of their energy each woman wastes every day on food. You can't see that one of them worries about her weight constantly, the other one is obsessed with eating healthily, and the third one hardly eats anything. Each one of them in their own way wastes nearly all of their daily energy on food. You also don't see what they are really hungry for. You don't see what made them obsessed with food in the first place." As Mary spoke, she leaned over and handed Melissa her glasses. "See for yourself."

Melissa looked at the three women again. They looked quite normal to her, and she thought that worrying about what they ate must be a pretty normal state of being for most women.

Wondering about how much of her own energy had been spent on dieting or not dieting, she perched Mary's glasses on her nose.

"Oh," was all she could muster. Gone were the three ordinary women having breakfast. One of them still looked somewhat like she had before, but her hair hung limply around her shoulders, and her eyes had sunk deep into their sockets. Her skin was ashen, and the veins in her hands bulged purple under her skin. The other two horrified Melissa so much that she had to close her eyes for a few seconds to brace herself for a proper look. When she did finally look more closely at them, she had to hold her breath to keep herself calm. Both women were shadows of what Melissa had seen before. Their skins were sickly grey, and their eyes were sunk so deeply into their heads that she almost couldn't see them anymore. As she listened, their fingers clicked like claws as they grasped at their spoons. Shoulders were hunched as if they carried a heavy weight, and their hair clung to their heads in lank tangles. As she watched, Melissa thought she could see wisps of smoke rising from their heads. Gasping for breath, she tore at the glasses. Flinging them onto the table, she stumbled outside in tears, barely making to the railing before she threw up.

"That all came from food?" Melissa asked timidly through tears a few minutes later as Mary joined her. She had stopped throwing up and was sitting on the floor of the balcony, using the railing for support.

"No, Melissa, you still don't understand," Mary said gently, sitting down beside her. "I've told you before, none of this has anything to do with food. Food is just the tool that we use to mask our other pain. People use food in many, many ways. They use it to feel like they are in control, they use it to numb, they use it to comfort, to fill a hole, or to protect themselves from the world. Food is just a thing. What you saw in there is the energy that is wasted by women worrying about food, but that energy is just displaced from something else. They are not feeding their real hunger; they are covering it up with food. Imagine how much better off women would be if they used all of that energy on living their lives instead of worrying about whether or not they should eat that piece of chocolate cake. Melissa, no matter how much food they put in their mouths, those women are starving. They are being eaten alive by their hunger."

"Why did you show me this?" Melissa finally asked.

"Because you were ready," Mary said. "There are a lot of people in there who would have nothing left if we showed them this. I was serious when I said that we sent people home. There is a reason why so many paths lead to this place. Nearly every single woman who begins this journey ends up here, but lots of them also get stalled here. Many women are so stuck in their relationship with food that they cannot see that there is more beyond this, so they never get any farther than the buffet. When you go out the other side of this building you will see just as many paths leading away, but you will see that not very many of them are as well travelled.

"Can I borrow your glasses again?" Melissa asked, taking a deep breath. Mary smiled as she handed them over. Melissa held them for a long time, turning them over and over in her hands.

"Was that what was coming out of their heads?" Melissa asked. "Was it their energy?"

"Yes," Mary said, getting up and stretching her back and motioning to Hannah that she needed to see her. "It was leaking out of them. That is what we keep track of on our computer. Now, I've got some work to do. Come find me when you have finished with the glasses."

Melissa remained where she was for a few minutes. She knew what she wanted to do with the glasses, but she took a long time to summon up the courage. Taking a deep breath, she got up and looped the silver chain around her neck. Looking out across the valley, she could see the way that she and the other girls had come. As she watched, a figure appeared at the edge of the woods. Melissa knew that the woman was wondering what the building meant. The woman walked across the clearing towards her. Sighing, Melissa turned her back on scene. She knew how all of this began. What she was concerned about was how it ended. Putting on the glasses, she turned and walked back through the door.

The scene in the dining room assaulted her. Everywhere she looked she saw walking pain and suffering. A figure moved ahead of her, bent almost double with the misery it carried. Nearly colliding with a woman carrying a tray, Melissa reached out instinctively to steady herself and found her hands clutching nothing but fabric and bone. As she touched the woman, she sensed an overwhelming feeling of loneliness. Melissa recoiled and the woman looked at her strangely. Apologizing, Melissa hurried past, bumping into tables and chairs as she went until she realized that in order to truly understand this, she needed to look these women in the eye.

"Excuse me," a woman said, nudging past to go towards the kitchen. Melissa was surprised when she saw the woman's back. It was straight. Melissa hurried to catch up with her, watching as the woman met someone that she knew and turned back in Melissa's direction, giving Melissa the chance to see her face. It wasn't grey. In fact, it was as healthy a face as Melissa had ever seen. Melissa gave a sigh of relief. So health was possible.

"Melissa!" A voice called to her. She had come within feet of her own table. Grace and Emma were waving at her.

"Where have you been?" Emma called. "We've been looking all over for you. We were scared you had left without us." Melissa felt bile burning her throat. Through the glasses, Emma's skin was a strange grey-green colour. Her eyes, like many of the other women's, were sunk deep into her head, and her cheekbones stood out in sharp defiance. Her hair hung limply around her face, and Melissa could feel shame emanating from her in waves.

"We waited to have breakfast so that we could have it with you," Grace said. Melissa forced herself to look at her face. Grace was so thin and grey she was nearly transparent. There was something spectral about her and her eyes had sunk so deeply into her head they could no longer be seen. Where with Emma Melissa had felt shame, with Grace she felt nothing but profound grief. Tears coursed down Grace's cheeks and fell onto her chest. So many tears had travelled down Grace's face that they had carved deep trails into her skin, and her sodden clothes clung to her body. Melissa suppressed a shudder but was unable to tear her gaze from Grace.

"What's wrong?" Grace asked. "You look really strange. Why are you still in your pyjamas?"

"Nothing's wrong," Melissa murmured, forcing a smile. "I couldn't sleep so I have been exploring. Let me go and get changed. You guys start without me!"

"Wait!" Grace said, getting up and walking around the table. "I found something that I thought you might like. I found it in my bag this morning, but I don't think I am going to need it. In her hand was a silver compass.

"Why won't you need this?" Melissa asked, gently holding the piece in her hand.

"I don't know. I just thought of you when I found it so I wanted you to carry it for me," Grace smiled. Melissa couldn't see the smile through the glasses; she could see only Grace's despair.

"Thank you," Melissa said, tucking the compass into her pocket. "You are right, I might need that someday." Without another word, Melissa turned and nearly ran from her table. Tears burned her eyes. How could Grace be so unhappy and hide it so well? Lost in her thoughts she bumped into someone else. Looking up, she saw another tear-carved face in front of her. This time the woman was so faded Melissa could see right through her. Stifling a cry, Melissa apologized and ran for the stairs, needing to see something for herself.

Safely inside her room, she rested her back against the door for a few minutes. When she was ready, she pushed open the bathroom door and walked forwards towards the sink. Forcing herself to remain calm, she leaned over and switched on the light beside the mirror. For a few seconds she couldn't see anything and then the image in front of her came into focus. Gasping, she took a few steps backwards. The reflection stepped back with her. Coming forward again, they met at the glass. Melissa reached a finger out to trace the lines of the reflected face. Her cheeks and jaw were sharply defined by the skin stretched greyly over her skull. Her eyes stood out coldly in their sockets, which were beginning to deepen, and dark circles showed nothing but fatigue and sadness. Her hair was lank and fell in dark grey tangles around her face, and her shoulders were beginning to stoop. Looking deeply into her own dull eyes, she whispered a question.

"What are you hungry for?" She asked, not expecting a reply. Giving herself as long as she needed, she stood quietly with the question between them until she began to feel the answer. Wave after wave of sadness crashed into her chest from deep inside. An overwhelming feeling of emptiness began to seep from every pore, making her skin slick and shiny. Clinging to the bathroom counter for support, she let the feeling of emptiness leak out of her until it soaked into her clothes and ran down her arms and legs and out onto the counter and the floor. Keeping her eyes locked on the ones in her reflection and not knowing what else to do, she stayed where she was, letting the tears and the emptiness mingle in sticky, salty puddles.

It felt like hours had gone by when she finally blinked and her reflection blinked back. Taking a deep breath, they both let go of the counter. Her fingers and shoulders ached and she began to rub them to get the circulation moving again. Taking a good, long look at herself again in the mirror, she saw that the Melissa that looked back looked a little straighter and a little less grey. Her hair was less tangled, and her eyes were clearer. Melissa smiled, and her reflection smiled back, knowing that she'd been seen.

Melissa took off the glasses.

Chapter Eight

"Sometimes we get to learn our lessons the easy way, and sometimes we have to do it the hard way. Some lessons require a nudge, and others require a slap on the back of the head. Just make sure that when you have learned a lesson that it stays learned. There's nothing worse that having to start all over again," Mary said, handing Melissa her bag. They were standing beside an open door at the back of the building. Outside Melissa could see many paths heading off into the woods and knew instinctively which one was hers.

"Is that what this is all about?' Melissa asked. "Learning lessons?"

"Something like that," Mary answered, smiling strangely.

"So when am I going to wake up?" Melissa asked, shouldering her bag.

"What do you mean?" Mary asked.

"When am I going to wake up in my bed and realize that this has all been a dream?" Melissa said, looking at the ground in discomfort.

"Melissa, I think that you will find that you are very much awake," Mary said, pinching her.

"But this can't be real!" Melissa exclaimed, laughing a little at the pinch and rubbing her arm.

"Why not?" Mary smiled.

"Because things keep appearing and disappearing. Because I saw my own reflection in your glasses. I don't know who I am here. I have got to be dreaming."

"Well, have you learned anything good so far?" Mary asked, shrugging her shoulders.

"I guess so," Melissa admitted, putting her hand on her throat.

"Well then, I suggest you just enjoy this dream as long as it lasts then," Mary smiled.

"Will you say goodbye to Emma and Grace for me?" Melissa asked.

"I will. I actually think I am going to go and have a talk with Emma today. Don't worry, they'll be fine," Mary assured her.

"Even Grace?" Melissa asked nervously.

"Even Grace," Mary answered. "It's going to take her a lot longer to be ready, but we will take care of her. Off you go now, I've got work to do." With that, Mary smiled and pushed the door open a little farther. Melissa walked through it and stepped onto her path. Turning to wave goodbye to Mary, she found the door behind her closed. She was alone. With no windows on this side of the building, she knew that no one would watch her go. Taking one last glance back, she entered the forest again.

"Oh thank goodness! Well, you took your time, didn't you? I've been waiting for you for ages!" Melissa jumped at the sound of the unexpected voice. Looking to her right, she was shocked to see Elle. Her long-lost companion was sitting on a log with one leg crossed over the other. Elle had obviously chosen not to wear the sensible shoes because one shiny black shoe was dangling off of her big toe. As she sat, she pumped her leg up and down, swinging the shoe precariously.

"What are you doing here?" Melissa laughed, delighted to see a familiar face.

"I told you, I was waiting for you," Elle sighed. "I thought you were never going to get out of there." With her shoe now on properly, she got up, dusted herself off, and stood with her hands on her hips, watching Melissa. "So, should we get going, or what?" Melissa laughed nervously and bowed at the waist, sweeping her arm out in an old fashioned, gallant gesture.

"After you," she smiled. Melissa wasn't sure how to take this strange turn of events. Elle slipped and slid on the uneven ground in front of her. Tall, thin and fashionable, today Elle was dressed in soft camel coloured trousers and a green cashmere v-neck sweater over a crisp, white shirt. Her hair, which was exactly the same colour as Melissa's, was pulled up into a fancy twist with just the right amount of it falling to frame her face. Even as inappropriately dressed as she was, in that moment, Melissa longed to be Elle.

"So what have you been doing since I last saw you?" Melissa asked, concentrating her attention on the ground.

"Mostly putting in time, waiting for you," Elle smiled.

"No! Come on, I'm sure you haven't just been sitting around," Melissa protested.

"Oh, no I've been busy," Elle answered vaguely. "So how many lessons do you think we are going to have to learn before we wake up?" Stumbling a little, she cursed under her breath.

"Are you sure we are sleeping?" Melissa asked quietly.

"Of course we are, don't be ridiculous," Elle stopped mid step to look at her. "Where else could we be? This sort of stuff doesn't happen in real life. Don't be ridiculous!"

"But what if…" Melissa started.

"No. You are being silly. This can't be real. You mean to tell me that you think our life is going on without us somewhere? I refuse to believe that."

"No," Melissa began, but Elle raised her eyebrows in a defiant look and Melissa fell silent again. The trees in this part of the woods were tall with large spaces between them, so there was a lot of light coming through to the forest floor. Most of the trees growing here were pine, so the ground beneath their feet was covered in orange needles, causing the women to slip and slide whenever the way became steep. Elle fell over several times, cursing as she dirtied one of her knees.

"This is ridiculous," Elle sputtered. "I have had enough of this." She stopped walking and plunked her bag roughly on the ground. Bent at the waist, she rummaged through the bag until a small cry told Melissa that she had found what she was looking for. Brushing her hair away from her face, she stood up holding a small black phone. Melissa laughed out loud.

"What?" Elle said. "Those bags seem to provide us with whatever we need. Well, I need a taxi. I have had enough roughing it."

"Are you crazy?" Melissa laughed. "We are in the middle of a forest. We are supposed to be on some deep spiritual mountain climbing journey or something. How is anyone going to get a taxi out here?"

"That, my dear girl, is not our problem!" Elle breezed as she called directory assistance. Melissa stood and looked around in disbelief.

"Yes, we would like a taxi please," Elle said. "No, I haven't got a pen, could you just patch me through? Thank you so much." Elle tapped her foot as she waited for an answer. "Yes, hello? I've had enough walking for the moment, could you come and get us please? No, frankly, I don't know where we are going, but I expect that the taxi driver will. It is that sort of place! No, I don't know where we are either, but something tells me you do. Thank you." Flipping the phone back into her bag, she smiled at Melissa in triumph. "Well, there's no sense in doing things the hard way is there?"

"Now what do we do?" Melissa said, barely hiding her confused laughter.

"We wait," Elle said. With that, they heard a whoosh and the sound of crackling pine needles. To Melissa's complete amazement, a taxi was driving through the trees towards them, and it wasn't an ordinary taxi. It was a black London cab!

"See, I told you," Elle said triumphantly. "We should remember that we don't have to always do what we think we are supposed to do. There are always options." Melissa pulled the door shut behind them. As Elle had predicted, the driver did not ask them where they were going. In fact, the driver did not even turn around as they started off through the woods.

"I wonder what's coming next," Melissa said, looking down as she found a place for her bag by her feet. Looking up, she felt the world shift on its axis beneath her. The feeling of travelling in an elevator wrapped around her again. Her stomach flip-flopped, and she reached out a hand to steady herself. As she regained her balance, she glanced out of the car windows. The trees were farther apart here, and she could have sworn that she could see a lamppost standing between two of them. Turning her head to look, she almost missed seeing the bright red mailbox peeking out between two trunks, but then she had to close her eyes to steady her stomach.

When she opened them again, the feeling of falling had passed and they were no longer in the woods. Somewhere in that moment when she wasn't paying attention, they had left the woods and were now driving along a residential street. Too shocked to ask how or why, she sat looking out the window with her mouth wide open. Lining the street on both sides were rows of small, white houses. Each house was trimmed in a different colour and there were flowers in the gardens, and fences around the lawns. As they drove by, she saw a woman watering a daffodil. Melissa tried to wave, but the woman didn't look up.

"How did we get here?" Melissa whispered to Elle.

"By taxi," Elle said, smiling. She knew what Melissa meant, but she didn't have an answer either. "Clearly we have turned a corner and ended up in the 1950s!" They both laughed uncomfortably. Melissa turned to watch the houses go by. In the middle of each lawn, a single flower grew. There were roses and daisies and carnations and peonies, but they were not growing in bushes or clumps, as she would have expected. Each grew on a single stalk and ended with a single bloom. She craned her neck to see more but she was distracted as the taxi came to a stop in front of one of the buildings. The taxi driver did not turn or speak or ask them for the fare. They sat for a few minutes before Elle shrugged and opened the door. Climbing out awkwardly, they stood beside the road. Melissa tried to thank the driver, but the cab pulled away before she could say anything.

"So what now?" Melissa asked. Elle shrugged her shoulders again and screwed up her face in confusion. Melissa looked around, feeling like she was looking at one of those 'spot-the-difference' puzzles that she had done as a child. Everything seemed so similar, but there were very subtle differences. As she turned and looked she realized that the house that they were in front of had one crucial difference from the others. It was the only one without a flower growing in the middle of the garden.

"It's this one," she said, stepping towards the white gate.

"How do you know?" Elle asked, her hands on her hips.

"I just know," Melissa answered. Behind her, Elle was chattering about shoulds and shouldn'ts, but Melissa knew where she had to go. She opened the gate and stepped through onto the lawn.

"Hello!" A voice greeted her. A small figure peered at her from around the corner of the house.

"Hello," Melissa smiled, squatting down so that the little girl would be less afraid of her. "I'm not sure, but I think I am supposed to be here."

"You're Melissa," the girl said with a smile. It wasn't a question.

"I am," Melissa nodded.

"I've got a message for you!"

"From who?" Melissa whispered.

"I'm supposed to tell you that before you are allowed to go any further you need to plant and grow a flower." The little girl walked forward as she spoke until she was standing directly in front of Melissa. She had dark red curly hair and wore a white dress with a green ribbon around her waist. The ends of the ribbon trailed in the grass. Her feet were bare.

"Like the ones in the middle of the other gardens?" Melissa asked, already knowing the answer. The girl nodded.

"There's stuff in the shed for growing flowers," the little one said, playing with one of her ears nervously.

"Which flower do I need to grow?" Melissa asked, still at eye level with the girl.

"Yours," the girl said, holding out her hand and offering Melissa a seed. Melissa held out her own hand and the girl tipped the seed from her palm to Melissa's. It was warm. The little girl smiled at her and cocked her head to one side, considering Melissa for a moment.

"I'd better give you these," she said, smiling. She reached into the pocket of her dress and brought out a few more seeds. "But just plant one at a time!" She tipped several other seeds into Melissa's other hand and smiled at her.

"Is there anything else I need to know?" Melissa asked.

"Nope. But don't forget, you have to plant and grow the flower before you can go," the little girl said, staring at her very seriously. Then she smiled again and turned and skipped across the lawn to the gate. "Bye!" She giggled as she left the garden. Melissa stayed where she was for a few moments, studying the seeds in her hands. Time slipped by in her mind. How long would it take to grow a flower? She poured all of the seeds into one hand and stirred them around with one finger. What was it that Mary had said about learning lessons?

"So what was that about planting a flower?" Elle stood behind Melissa with growing impatience. "Was she kidding? We don't have time for this! We should be getting to the top of some mountain somewhere so that we can go home, not wasting time waiting for flowers to grow!"

"I know. I am as impatient as you are to get home," Melissa sighed and stood. "But this journey doesn't seem to be about our agenda, does it?" Elle sighed impatiently again. Still holding the seeds, Melissa turned towards the house. With no doubt in her mind that they were supposed to go inside, she stepped through the door, calling hello as she went. There was no answer, but she hadn't expected one.

"So what do we do now?" Elle asked. They were standing in the kitchen. It was painted soft creamy green. The counters and the appliances were all white. The kitchen table and chairs were white as well, but they had silver legs. Across the room from where they stood, a door opened into a living room.

"Let's look around a little bit and then I guess we should plant one of these seeds. I'm thirsty though, I'm going to get myself a drink of water." Melissa opened her hand and dumped the seeds into a little pile on the corner on the counter that was closest to the door. Opening the cupboards she could see that they were well stocked. The refrigerator was full of vegetables and fruits and cheese and milk. In the cupboard to the left of the sink she found the glasses. Turning the cold tap on full and letting it run for a moment, she absently held her fingers under the running water as she stared out the window that was above the sink, suddenly feeling like her mother.

Filling her glass, she turned off the water. On the windowsill above the sink sat a green ceramic frog holding a sponge in its wide mouth. Melissa stared at it for a moment and then chuckled to herself, realizing that her grandmother had had a similar frog in her kitchen. Both her mother and her grandmother had invaded her thoughts in the last few moments and Melissa realized that although she hadn't really thought about them in a long time, they were with her now in this kitchen.

Rinsing the glass out, she rubbed her fingers around the rim, and turned it upside down on the draining board. Not wanting to meet any more memories, she dried her hands on her hips rather than looking for a tea towel and went looking for Elle.

The living room was full of gloom. Thick net curtains blocked most of the light from the window. Beige carpet and heavily stuffed dark burgundy furniture filled the room. Against the wall beside the window was a glass-fronted cabinet filled with china and figurines. A coffee table squatted in the middle of the room, holding a doily and a candy-filled glass dish. To her right a hallway ran away from the room she was in, so she followed it. The first door on her left was open and showed a bright yellow bathroom. To her right there was a simple bedroom decorated in pink. On either side at the end of the corridor there were two more bedrooms. Elle stood in the one on Melissa's left. It held a large bed and was decorated in soft cream. The one on Melissa's right had a bed in it, but it was also clearly used as a study. Two of the walls were lined with books, and there was a desk under a window that looked out onto the back yard.

"Do you mind if I sleep in here?" Elle called, sitting on the side of the cream coloured bed. Melissa replied that she didn't as she opened the last door. It was at the end of the corridor between the bedroom doors. Behind it, she found a laundry room and the door to the back yard.

"I'm going to just go outside and have a look around," Melissa called back to Elle. The laundry room was thick with the smell of fabric softener and the air was soft and slippery as she walked through it. Just outside the back door she froze. There, in the distance, was her mountain. She hadn't seen it since she had gone back into the forest at Lola's cottage. She sat down on the porch for a few minutes to look at it, nerves prickling under her skin. Melissa had almost forgotten about the mountain, and she was soon drawn towards the fence. Holding onto two of the pickets, she kept staring at the mountain. She knew that in order to get home she needed to reach it, but it still looked so far away. On the other side of the fence from where she stood, a path began. It started just in front of her and headed off in the direction of the mountain. She debated climbing over the fence, but she knew somehow that it wouldn't work. With one last look she turned away. The mountain would be there when she was ready.

In the bottom left hand corner of the garden stood a shed. Sure enough, it was full of gardening supplies. Trowels and shovels and bags of fertilizer waited for her to give them a purpose. A watering can, pairs of rubber boots and gloves and even a sun hat were all there ready for her to put them to good use. Cobwebs hung thickly from every corner, but it still reminded her of a shed her grandparents had had when she was a little girl. Dried potting soil, various screws and nails, half-empty flower pots and tools lay scattered across the surface of a table at the back of the shed. A small window, nearly hidden by a thick layer of cobwebs and grime had been cut into the wall behind the table. The sill was covered in tiny insect bodies and filth. Through the window she could make out the outline of the mountain in the distance, but it was distorted and discoloured.

"Okay. Tools," Melissa said firmly. Her voice fell onto the table with the other debris. On one shelf she found a pair of gloves, so caked in dirt they stood to attention. On another shelf sat a slightly younger pair, and she put these into a bucket with a trowel and a small bag of fertilizer. She had been hoping for some instructions of some sort, but they were not there. Taking the bucket in one hand and a watering can in the other, she stepped outside.

Instead of going back through the house, Melissa went around. A small, round, empty flowerbed waited for her in the front yard. Melissa realized that the last time she had planted anything had been in school when she was about seven. They had planted seeds in little paper cups and put them on the windowsill to grow. No matter how hard she tried, she couldn't remember if her seed had grown. Her only memory was of the row of paper cups sitting in the sun.

Gloves on, she used the trowel to dig a small hole in the centre of the bed and scooped in a little bit of fertilizer. Getting up, she wiped her knees and went back into the kitchen to get her seeds. They were still sitting on the counter. What had the little girl said? Melissa remembered being given one seed first and then the others, but she didn't know which seed had been first. Taking off her gloves, she stirred the seeds with her finger, noticing that they were all different. Shrugging, she picked up the roundest one. Holding it in her palm, she was amazed to find that it was still warm.

Back on her knees in the garden, she opened her fingers and looked at the seed again. It felt like magic on her palm. "From little acorns," she whispered. It was amazing to her that something was going to grow from this little seed. Holding it up between two fingers, she squinted at it.

"Good luck," she whispered, and put it into the hole. With bare hands she gently scooped the dirt back into the hole. Patting the earth, she sat back again, admiring her handiwork. Taking her watering can to the sink in the kitchen, she saw that the little green frog was still watching her with his mouth open.

"What are you looking at?" She asked.

Seed planted, Melissa piled her tools just inside the kitchen door ready for the next time she went out to check on the garden. Job done, she was at a bit of a loss about what to do next. Looking in on Elle, she found her sound asleep on top of the big cream bed. After covering Elle with a blanket, Melissa moved into her own room. There were plenty of books she could read in here if she needed to pass the time. Sighing, she looked down at her dirty hands and smiled. There were plenty of books she could read after she had enjoyed a very long, very hot bath.

Chapter Nine

"Have I mentioned how ridiculous this is?" Elle asked, sitting on the front step of the house. Melissa was on her hands and knees in the garden giving the plant some more fertilizer.

"Yes, you have mentioned it," Melissa replied through gritted teeth. Elle had been mentioning her displeasure for the last few days.

"Well, why don't we go have a look and see whether there is another way out of here?" Elle asked, resting her head in the palm of her hand.

"We'll do that tomorrow," Melissa replied, anxious to make Elle a little happier. Melissa was determined to do as she'd been told. She knew that they needed to make this flower grow before they could leave, so she had been dutifully watering and fertilizing and watching its every movement. Melissa had been watching when the small green shoot had first poked its head above the ground and she had excitedly called Elle. Together they had been amazed at how quickly they had managed to get the seed to grow. Every day it had grown steadily taller, unfurling itself into a straight, strong stalk, and Melissa spent most of each day watching or tending to the little sprout in some way. Elle had soon become bored of the whole thing.

"Come on, let's go now," Elle whined. "I'm so bored of this."

"I can't go now," Melissa sighed, dusting herself off as she got up. I need to make sure it is safe for the night."

"Safe from what?" Elle asked.

"Anything," Melissa replied.

"Oh, for goodness sake," Elle sighed, crossing her arms, but staying on the porch. She continued to complain and moan but Melissa pretended not to hear.

Melissa could see that they were getting close to having a bloom. The stalk had finished growing, so surely the flower would not be far behind. All she wanted was for the flower to bloom so that they could be on their way. She had never grown a flower before. In fact, thinking about it, she realized that apart from in school, she had never grown anything before. There had been a spider plant in her life in university. The friend who had given it to her had told her that spider plants cleaned the air in a room and made it better to breathe or something. Well, it had died and she hadn't really had a plant since then.

Over the next few days, Melissa kept a vigil. She watched and watered and fertilized and tended and weeded until her knees and back ached, and her hands cramped, stopping only to eat and sleep. One morning, she was elated to find that her plant had developed a large bud in the night. Dancing around the yard, she announced to Elle that it was finally going to bloom.

"Well thank goodness for that!" Elle sighed as she came out onto the porch. With a cup of coffee in one hand, she used the other to balance her as she sat down.

"It's going to bloom before we know it!" Melissa circled the little plant again. "Maybe I should water it a little more."

For the next four days, they watched for any sign of bloom-ing. Melissa watered and fertilized and sang to it. She looked up and down the road at other gardens to try to figure out what sort of flower she was going to get and sat vigil at its side on most days, but was always disappointed by nightfall. Nothing was happening. She wondered if maybe her flower was stuck. There didn't seem to be any other explanation for things not moving more quickly.

"Aren't we going yet?" Elle asked on the morning of the fifth day. They were outside again, and Elle had toast in her hand this time. "I am so sick of waiting for this thing to bloom. Maybe we should help it along."

"I was thinking the same thing," Melissa nodded. "It's strange that it is taking so long. I wondered yesterday if it was stuck. Maybe we should just help it a little." Melissa took the bud in her hands and with the smallest movement, she slid one fingernail under the outermost layer of petals. She looked up at Elle, her heart beating quickly. Elle shrugged, so Melissa used her fingernail to open the bud up just a little bit. Sure enough, it popped open beneath her fingers. It didn't bloom, but it had finally opened.

"I won't go any further," Melissa whispered as she let go of the bud. It stood back up on its own. They could just see the deep, dark red of the petals.

"Come and have some breakfast," Elle called. "Nothing is going to happen in the next five minutes." Melissa followed Elle back into the house, feeling unsettled about the whole thing. Filling the kettle for a cup of tea, she looked out the window and let out a scream, letting the kettle fall into the sink with an enormous crash. Elle came rushing back into the kitchen to see what had happened, but Melissa was already running out the door.

"NO!" Her strangled cry filled the house and echoed up and down the street as she fell to her knees in the garden. The bud had flopped over and was hanging limply on one side. The outer layer had curled away and on the ground lay three deep red petals. As they watched, another petal fell, landing softly on top of the others. Melissa tried in vain to hold the flower's head up straight again, but it was no use. It was dead.

"You must have watered it too much," Elle said, looking at her fingernails.

"How could you say that?" Melissa seethed, her teeth clenched in frustration and disappointment. "Can't you see we have to start all over again?" Tears filled her eyes, and she sat on the ground to watch her flower drop another petal.

"Well, what do you want me to say?" Elle flounced back into the house, leaving Melissa alone.

"I'm sorry," Melissa whispered to what was left of her flower. "I'm sorry I tried to force you." Not knowing what else to do, she watched it for a long time as it withered before her eyes. Before long, the petals had all fallen, and the stalk had sagged to the ground. With an aching heart, Melissa got up and went into the house. She had had enough of today. Through the window above the desk in her room she could see her mountain. Groaning she crawled into bed and pulled the covers over her head. Maybe if she went to sleep now, she would wake up and this would all be over. Maybe she would wake up in her own bed and have breakfast in her own kitchen and this would fade away into a fuzzy memory. Hiding under the covers, she could have been anywhere. She fell asleep hoping to wake up somewhere else.

It was dark when Melissa opened her eyes. As her eyes adjusted, she made out the outline of the window over the desk and she flopped back onto her pillow in disgust as she remembered where she was. Having gone to bed in the middle of the day she had missed dinner, and her stomach rumbled as soon as she thought of food. It would never let her go back to sleep without giving it something to fill it so she pushed the covers back. Still wearing the clothes that she had put on yesterday, she kicked off her shoes and padded softly out to the kitchen.

While she was adding milk to a bowl of cereal, she glanced through the kitchen window. Putting the milk jug down, she rolled her eyes in disgust as she saw the flower lying on the ground. Back in her room, she sat cross-legged on her bed and leaned back against the headboard, looking out the window to where the mountain stood, just visible in the growing dawn. Her thoughts tumbled through her head and she whispered them to the waiting mountain.

"Maybe I've been going about this all wrong. Maybe I don't need to find you. Maybe I could go home if I just turned around and went back. I've had enough. I don't remember what it was I wanted to change when I started all of this. I'm sure I was happy in my life before. I need to get back to my life and sort it all out. I can't believe that my journey depends on planting a stupid seed. Ooh, I have had enough!" She threw her pillow towards the window. It landed thickly on the desk. Her cereal bowl was still in one hand, but she wasn't hungry anymore. She put it on her bedside table and pulled the covers up over her legs.

"I've had enough," she whispered at the mountain. It didn't answer.

"Well, I think that we should plant another seed just in case there is no way out and then spend our time trying to find another way," Elle said through a mouthful of toast. "That way all of our options are covered." Melissa nodded, not wanting to think of all of the work that went into starting all over again, but Elle's suggestion made sense. She just wouldn't put so much effort into taking care of the flower again.

"Okay, let's go out after breakfast and plant another seed. Once we've done that we can go for a walk." Melissa was tired despite her long sleep the day before. She had sat up with the mountain for a long time before she'd fallen back into a fitful doze and had woken up this morning grumpy and irritable. Scooping last night's cereal into the garbage, she made herself a piece of toast and jam.

With a pang of remorse, Melissa pulled the dead flower from the dirt. Its roots had been good and strong, and it took her a few minutes to free them. She didn't want to throw it in the garbage, but she didn't know where else to put it. Finally, she walked around to the back of the house and put it on the other side of the fence, behind the shed. Dusting off her hands, she turned and walked back to the front garden. Kneeling down, she dug a hole with her trowel. When the hole was big enough, she pulled a seed from her pocket and dropped it into the hole, scooping dirt over it, patting it down, and adding a bit of water for good measure.

"Well that's done," she said. Leaving the watering can and the trowel on the grass, she went back into the house to get Elle.

Elle proved to be good company when she wasn't frustrated about waiting for a seed to grow. They began exploring their neighbourhood. Having spent so much of her energy growing the last flower, Melissa did not seem to have much left for the new blossom. Perhaps she had over watered the last one. There was also a niggling suspicion that by attempting to force it to bloom, she had ended its life. From the moment she had patted the earth around this seed, and given it a little water, she basically ignored it. Every morning when they left, she would look over at it and see that it had grown a little more in the night. Despite her lack of attention, it appeared to be doing well, so she continued to let it be.

They would get up, have breakfast, get ready and go out for long walks. They figured that there had to be another way home, so they walked as far as they could in both directions, Elle chattering all the way. Melissa found that as long as Elle was chattering she was not worrying about the seed or the journey or never getting home. As they walked along the street, they would look at the various houses and try to decide who lived there. They made up lives and careers and families for some of the houses, but they never saw another soul. Every now and then they would hear a faint whisper on the wind that sounded like someone else was out in their garden working, but despite looking everywhere, they didn't see anyone. Melissa remembered seeing a woman working in a garden on the way in, but she couldn't remember which house it was.

"What was it?" Elle asked one day as they were walking home.

"What was what?" Melissa asked back, absently tapping her hand along the tops of the fence posts as she moved past them.

"What flower was it that we were growing? You can see here that there seems to be dozens of different types of flowers growing in the front gardens. I just wondered which one we were trying to grow." Elle paused at the gate to one of the houses. In the middle of this garden grew an enormous sunflower. Melissa thought back to the flower that she had just grown. She had no idea what sort it had been. Her days had been filled with it, she had lovingly tended it and spent all of her time looking after it, and she had no idea what it had been. The petals had been red, she knew that much. But she had been so intent on growing it, she hadn't paid attention to what it really was.

"I think it was a tulip," she lied. Elle was content with the answer. The stood and admired the sunflower for a few moments longer, then Elle sighed and turned for home. Melissa followed her quietly, trying to ignore the blossoms in everyone else's garden.

Arriving at their gate, Elle stepped through and walked towards the house, eager to be home and have something to eat. Melissa followed, still lost in thought. Out of habit more than anything, she flicked her gaze over to the middle of the garden. It took her a moment to take in what she saw. When she realized what had happened, she stepped towards the little flower and sagged to the ground beside it, tears streaming down her face.

The little plant had barely reached a foot tall and had not yet produced a bud. It was still standing up straight in the middle of its mound of earth, but where it had been lush and green the last time she had looked at it, now it was shrivelled and brown. Melissa took a leaf between her fingers and snapped it off. Holding it to her mouth, she crumbled it into sharp pieces against her lips. Hot tears covered her cheeks, but she could not explain the depth of her grief. She felt guilty for not paying more attention to this delicate creature. She was disappointed that home was so far away again. But why was she crying so deeply? Why did it bother her so much that she would never know what sort of flower this had been?

Wiping her nose with a dirty hand, she took a shuddering breath and came up onto her knees determined not to wait another day to plant again. Digging at the earth, she easily pulled up the little plant. Its roots had been weak. She held it for a moment and then got up and carried it to the fence behind the shed.

"I'm sorry," she whispered, placing it with the first flower before she turned and walked back into the house. Elle was nowhere to be seen. Melissa took another seed from the pile on the kitchen counter and took it out to the garden. Again she dug a small hole. Again she placed the seed gently on the dirt. Again she gently scooped earth over it and gave it a little water. She couldn't believe that she was starting all over again, but she had the distinct feeling that time was running out: she needed to get this seed in the ground. This time she would make sure she found out what flower the seed produced.

"Is that thing never going to bloom?" Elle was sitting on the front porch again. Melissa rolled her eyes, tired of Elle's constant negativity. Melissa had begun to enjoy spending time in the garden. She had found other packages of seeds in the shed and had spent some time planting them in the empty garden in front of the fence. These seeds had taken quickly, and one day she had woken up to find an enchanting expanse of sweet peas blooming in the early morning sun. Their sweet fragrance filled every corner of the garden. Melissa's time was now shared between tending the slow growing bloom in the centre and the riotous bunch around the edges. She was also spending time looking through the books that lined the walls of her room, often taking them with her into the garden or into the bath. Things around her were blooming, and she was determined to do it right it this time.

"Is that thing never going to bloom?" Elle was beginning to sound like a broken record. Melissa was about to give a sharp answer when she noticed a small bee climbing out of one of the sweet peas in front of her. Holding her breath, she watched it fly blissfully from bloom to bloom. Her heart beat madly in her chest, and she realized that this was the first sign of animal life she had seen since she started this journey. She remembered the silence of the forest and the stark cleanliness of the food hall. No birds had been singing in the trees, and no flies had been buzzing around plates of food. Melissa listened rapturously to the buzzing of the solitary bee and her heart sang in reply.

"Did you hear what I said?" Elle said, still sitting on the porch.

"Oh, it'll bloom," Melissa replied with a silly smile. She turned around to look at the flower in question. It had grown a little more in the night, and it was now over two feet tall. A bud was only just beginning to form at the top of the stem. As she watched, she could have sworn it shuddered a little. She smiled again and turned back to her weeding. It was blooming all right; they just couldn't see it yet.

Encouraged by the growth of her sweet peas, Melissa decided to dig a little deeper in the shed. After a bit of housekeeping, the shed was a little easier to navigate. On one of the topmost shelves she found some more seeds stored in large glass jars. None of them were labelled, so she pulled the jars down and left them on the worktable to study them more closely. Looking even higher, she found a garden fork and was surprised at her level of delight over this find. It was like that little bee had brought the nectar of the flowers up and pollinated her with it and she felt revived and replenished.

As the days passed, her little garden began to flourish. She had planted some more of the seeds she had found in the shed, and now blooms surrounded the house. More and more of her days were spent kneeling on the ground, pulling weeds from the earth. Melissa made sure that the first thing she cared for in the morning and the last thing she cared for at night was the bloom in the middle. Only then would she turn her attention outwards, and the bud grew bigger every day.

It was while she was washing out a glass one morning that she had the distinct feeling that something was different. Leaving the glass on the draining board, she went outside. The heart that had been pounding skipped a beat. The little girl was back on the lawn, dancing all by herself on the grass, the green ribbon trailing along behind her. When she saw Melissa, she stopped and smiled, gesturing towards the centre of the garden with one hand.

"You did it," she smiled, running over to where Melissa stood. "You did it!"

Melissa couldn't speak. The flower had bloomed in the night into an enormous dark purple poppy. Falling to her knees in front of it, she saw that it was beautiful. Staring deeply into its heart, lusciously purple petals greeted her. Smiling a soft smile, she relaxed backwards until she was sitting on the ground. She had done it.

"It's time to go" the little girl said, coming to stand beside Melissa. Melissa looked up at her with tears in her eyes.

"But what about my flowers? I can't just leave them. They need me."

"You have already done everything you need to do for them. They will keep blooming here while you go on," the little girl said. Melissa looked around at the beautiful garden she had created. As she sat silently, she heard the buzzing of another bee. Scanning the garden eagerly, she saw it flying towards her. As she watched, it landed on her poppy and disappeared into the heart of the flower. A few moments later it emerged and flew drunkenly towards one of her sweet peas, soon disappearing inside the bloom.

"Okay. I think I am ready to go," she said quietly.

Chapter Ten

It wasn't until she was almost finished packing that Melissa remembered Elle. She had been so lost in her thoughts about her garden she had completely forgotten that there was more to worry about than just how her plants would do without her. She was amazed at how far Elle had fallen from her thoughts. Feeling guilty, she left her packing and knocked on Elle's door.

"Elle? Are you awake?" Melissa knocked harder. Getting no reply, she opened the door a crack. Elle was still in bed. She lay on her side with her back to the door. Melissa called her name quietly again. When she still did not get an answer, Melissa sat on the edge of the bed and gently shook Elle with one hand. Finally, Elle opened her eyes and looked at Melissa strangely. Melissa couldn't help but feel like Elle was looking through her.

"Good morning," Elle said, rolling onto her back and stretching tiredly. "What's wrong?"

"Nothing's wrong," Melissa answered with a smile. "It bloomed."

"Oh," Elle answered listlessly. "That's good. Does that mean we're going?" She yawned and stretched again. Melissa was confused. She had been expecting a bit more excitement.

"Uh, yeah. We're going as soon as we've packed. How soon can you be ready?" Melissa asked, getting up from the bed and putting her hands on her hips, not in the mood for Elle's attitude.

"Well, just let me have a shower and something to eat, and I'll be ready to go," Elle said, pulling herself into a sitting position and pulling her hair away from her face. "Who knows when we will be able to have another shower."

Melissa smiled tightly and left Elle to get herself ready, going back into her room to finish packing. Examining the contents of her bag, she vaguely remembered putting her shiny red shoes into her bag, but they were nowhere to be seen. Although the bag was open, no food or drink appeared. Laughing quietly to herself, she started putting her clothes into the bag. Nothing on this trip had made sense so far, why was she trying to make it happen now?

"What's funny?" Elle asked, leaning on the doorframe, her hair and body wrapped in towels.

"Nothing," Melissa answered. "I was just thinking about the time I found hot Macaroni and Cheese in my bag."

"What?" Elle said, wrinkling her brow in confusion.

"Never mind. Are you almost ready?"

"Why won't you tell me the story?" Elle whined.

"Because it's a long story and it's not important. Will you get ready please?" Melissa closed her bag with a tug, feeling badly for snapping at Elle. They hadn't been spending very much time together over the past little while. Without the garden to tend she expected that Elle had been a little bit bored with their situation so she decided she'd tell Elle the story once they were on their way.

"I wonder where we are going next," Melissa called out.

"I don't know. The mountain doesn't look too far from here. Maybe we are almost there," Elle called back. There was relief in her voice and Melissa felt even guiltier for snapping at her.

"Listen, I think that you should have this," Elle said, standing at the door to Melissa's room holding a woollen shawl in her hands.

"Why, don't you need it?" Melissa asked, puzzled.

"Well, no, I don't think so. I think you might need it someday and that you should carry it." Elle folded the shawl over and over again as she spoke. Melissa wrinkled her forehead in confusion, but she reached for the shawl.

"If you ever need it back, just let me know," she said cheerily, stuffing the shawl into the top of the bag.

"I will," Elle said quietly.

Melissa wanted to spend a few more precious minutes in her garden and Elle wanted to see the flower blooming, so they had some lunch in the garden before they left. Elle 'oohed' and 'aahed' over the colour of the poppy and told Melissa how clever she was for making it work this time. After finishing their lunch, they cleaned up the kitchen together. Hanging the dishcloth over the edge of the sink to dry, Melissa looked at the little green frog sitting on the windowsill and thought about her grandmother again. Reaching forward, she stroked her finger along the line of the frog's mouth and finished by rubbing his head.

"Goodbye," she whispered. "Be good."

They left through the back door. Melissa went out last, pulling the door firmly shut behind them. Shouldering their bags for the first time in ages, they walked away from the house. A gate had appeared in the fence. Melissa looked back at the house behind them. She would miss this place and the garden that she had created. Putting her right hand into her pocket, she smiled softly to herself. There had been one seed left on the kitchen counter this morning, and she hadn't been able to leave it behind. Someday she would know what it was to become.

Without a word, they stepped out of the garden and onto the path. Melissa could feel the difference under their feet immediately. Things shifted and moved around her and she had the sensation of falling though she hadn't gone anywhere. She had felt this feeling several times before so she knew what was coming: something was about to change. She sensed the temperature dropping around them, and by the time her stomach settled, the house had disappeared, and nothing but fields stretched out around them in every direction. Melissa was disappointed: she had hoped for more.

They spent the better part of the day following the path through fields. Nothing grew in these fields except grass, and even that was patchy. They could see the mountain in the distance, but it did not seem to ever get any closer. The ground grew harder and harder beneath their feet, and the patchy sandy fields they walked through were studded with rocks. They found that they had to concentrate on the ground in front of them in order to stay on their feet.

"Will you tell me again why we left our house?" Elle joked as they climbed up onto a mound of rocks. Melissa smiled and stopped walking, pausing to get some water out of her bag. Drinking deeply, she sighed and sat down for a moment to rest. Elle followed suit.

"It doesn't seem to be getting any closer does it?" Melissa squinted at the mountain in the distance, shimmering on the horizon. The air tingled on their skin and the rocks they were sitting on were cold and rough. This was no place to rest for very long. The water Melissa was drinking was making her feel sick and she longed for a cup of peppermint tea, but didn't look into her bag for any. Peppermint tea needed to be sipped from a china cup in a snug, warm chair. She wondered how long it would be before she found a place like that.

They continued on for most of the afternoon. At Melissa's insistence, Elle had changed her shiny shoes for something a little more practical. Melissa was worried about her. Elle had lost much of her sass. The more Melissa took control of the situation the quieter Elle became. There were even a few times when, looking at Elle, Melissa had the strongest feeling that she could almost see through her. Melissa felt guilty, but she knew deep in her heart that the choices she was making were the right ones, no matter what Elle tried to tell her. Melissa smiled gently to herself. Elle was just trying to keep them safe, she thought. Perhaps she should be a little bit gentler with her.

Melissa wondered if they were ever going to be travelling in the forest again. Looking around at the rocky terrain, she realized how much she missed trees. This landscape was foreign to her, and the sharper the stones got, the tenser she felt. They had to be on constant alert for loose rocks and slippery surfaces. They had been walking like this for several days and the path continued to rise up in front of them with no end in sight. Somewhere in the middle of the third day they had stopped talking to each other out of sheer concentration.

"What's that?" Melissa asked. She stood absolutely still for a moment: something was different.

"What's what?" Elle asked, coming to a stop beside her. Melissa cocked her head to one side and listened, sniffing the air. The air around them seemed to be grumbling under its breath. The sound wasn't loud enough to hear properly, but she could feel the echo deep in her chest.

"Where do you think it's coming from?" Elle asked, looking around them.

"I don't know," Melissa said, starting to move up the path again. Elle was clearly reluctant to follow. When Melissa ignored her resistance Elle sighed and hurried to catch up.

They continued on for a few hours in silence. The way got steeper as they went and soon they were climbing. Hand over hand and foot after foot they made their way along the path. They climbed higher and higher and then the path levelled off and they were walking on flat ground again. Melissa could feel her body and her mind breathe a sigh of relief, but she could still sense the strange rumbling. It seemed to be coming from the ground beneath her feet. She stopped and listened again.

"Look!" Elle cried with relieved excitement. Melissa turned to look around and saw a plume of smoke in the distance. Melissa sniffed again. It wasn't the smoke that she could smell, but she was certainly glad to see it. They started walking along the path again, their steps hurried with anticipation. Melissa had done this enough times now to be apprehensive about what would happen next. She hoped that whatever it was, it was friendly.

It wasn't long before they could smell wood smoke. The closer they got, the more it wrapped its arms around them, pulling them over each rise. At the top of one of the hills, they were completely surrounded by smoke for a moment and then, just as quickly as it had come, the smoke let go of them and whirled back up into the sky, disappearing on the wind. They were left standing in front of a large stone house. Made of the same rough grey stone as the land it sat on, the house looked like it had been carved out of the ground. Even though it was only just dusk, lights were glowing out of all of the windows, giving Melissa the impression of a grinning Halloween pumpkin. Laughter could be heard echoing through its stone rooms and escaping through the windows and up the chimney.

"Well come on, let's go in!" Elle said, smiling properly for the first time in three days. Melissa was not as excited. She had seen all of this before. Looking down at her feet, she saw that her path did not lead up to the front door. It led past the house.

"I don't know. I think I would like to go just a little farther and see what is up ahead," she said.

"Why?" Elle said wearily. "It's going to be dark soon. We have come all of this way. We can start again in the morning."

"Just come with me for a minute. The path seems to stop just down there," Melissa said, pointing past the house. Not waiting for an answer, she walked a little farther along the path. The sound in her chest vibrated more deeply with every step she took. The path slanted upwards again and she scrambled up the hill before stopping short at the top. Her breath caught in her throat and she made a strangled noise. Elle came panting up behind her to see what had caused such a reaction and her mouth fell open in surprise.

"Well I didn't expect that," Elle said, putting one hand on her head. In front of them yawned a vast rocky ravine. The sound that Melissa had been feeling came from the foaming rapids far below them. The path continued down as five steps carved into stone, and then it took the form of a narrow bridge that spanned the entire width of the ravine. Melissa sniffed the air. The breath that came from the rapids beneath was intoxicating. The energy from the space and the tumbling water pulled at her feet. She knew without any doubt that she was meant to cross the bridge.

"Elle, I am sorry, but I think that we need to keep going," Melissa said, screwing her face up apologetically.

"What?" Elle said, turning a confused face toward Melissa. "But I really think we should stop and spend the night here. We can have a good sleep and start again in the morning."

"I can't stop there," Melissa said, looking back at the stone house. It promised a warm bed and a rest, but she had stopped for a rest before and had ended up staying more than three months. No. Her path lay across the bridge. She could not listen to Elle. She needed to go now.

"I'm so sorry Elle," Melissa said, looking across the ravine. "I know you are just trying to take care of me, but I can't stay there tonight. I can go on alone if you want, I don't need you to take care of me anymore." Melissa turned and looked at Elle's face and was startled by how much it had changed in the past few days. It looked softer, like it was slightly out of focus, and Melissa could have sworn that she could almost see the path behind straight through her. She hadn't actually been paying Elle much attention at all since their last conversation in the garden. As Melissa had grown in confidence, she simply hadn't needed Elle anymore.

Elle nodded sadly and looked at Melissa with a strange look in her eyes. Without saying a word, she motioned for Melissa to go ahead. Melissa's heart started to beat with excitement. The bridge looked dangerous, but she was not afraid. Sheer cliffs stood sentry on the far side, but even that did not deter her. Climbing down the five steps and without a backward glance, she stepped onto the bridge.

It was a slow crossing. There were no handrails and the surface of the bridge was slick with water from the mist rising from the rapids. Melissa glanced back once to see how Elle was doing and was surprised to see that Elle had made it half way across but had stopped and was standing watching her go. One hand raised in a wave, Elle suddenly looked as soft and grey as the mist that swirled around her feet. Melissa stopped walking and turned around carefully to ask her what was wrong, glancing down briefly to make sure her footing was sound. When she looked up again, Elle had disappeared.

Heart thumping, she frantically scanned the bridge. Night was falling and she could no longer see the far side. She knew in her heart that Elle could not have gotten to the other side so quickly, and decided that Elle must have fallen off of the bridge. Screaming Elle's name, Melissa dropped to her knees on the slippery surface and strained her eyes at the churning water below. She called out for Elle again and again, gripping the sides of the bridge for support as she searched the water, the bridge, and the far side of the ravine, hoping that somehow her friend would magically reappear. Things like that happened here. People had disappeared and things had appeared before, maybe this was one of those times. Maybe she hadn't fallen at all. Surely Melissa would have heard her cry out? Elle's name left her lips again and again, and she sank to a sitting position on the bridge. It was slimy and cold under her legs but she didn't notice. Shaking her head she sat and stared into space. If she waited long enough, Elle would reappear.

Dusk turned into darkness and finally the cold seeped into Melissa's shock. When she realized that she was shivering uncontrollably she painfully and carefully got to her feet. Looking back across the ravine at where she had come from she knew that she could not go back. No matter how painful it was to admit, Melissa knew that she had to cross the bridge. Picking up her bag from where it had fallen she carefully picked her way to the other side of the ravine. It was so dark on the other side, she could not go any further. Opening her bag, she pulled out a change of clothes and her grey sweater. A little searching found a few pieces of wood and she managed to light a meagre fire. Sitting and watching the dancing flames, she allowed grief to overwhelm her. She had no idea what she was supposed to do next. Sobbing and utterly exhausted, she curled up on the ground and cried herself to sleep.

Chapter Eleven

There were always a few seconds when she first opened her eyes in the morning when she forgot to be sad. For a moment or two she would sigh and stretch and wonder what the day held for her, and then the memories would come piercing back into her and she would be crushed with pain all over again. Once the initial grief and guilt had passed she would then feel guilty for forgetting about her friend or for enjoying life for that brief speck of time. Grief and guilt seemed to felt like the only constants in her life – apart from those first few seconds of every day.

Melissa had spent a few days lingering around the edge of the ravine. Facing the other side and cupping her hands around her mouth so that the sound would carry as far as possible, she would shout Elle's name until her throat was sore and her voice hoarse. No one ever came out of the house to answer her and Elle did not reappear. All she wanted to do was curl up on the ground and cry but she knew that if she let herself do that she would never stop. There were many years worth of tears already stuck in her throat, so she knew she could hold these new ones in too. Steeling herself, she decided to get moving again.

The ache in her heart made it so heavy that every step was exhausting. No matter how much she pushed forward the ache in her heart pulled her back in the direction of her grief. Her throat was tight and sore and sometimes she had to remind herself to breathe. The way was rocky and cold and she kept stumbling, often ending up on the ground in tears. Her tears were no longer just for Elle. Instead of receding, her grief seemed to grow with each passing day. Every tear she had ever held back, every memory she had ever repressed was now fighting to get out, and it was becoming too much to bear.

After travelling like this for some time she realized that if she concentrated every ounce of her attention on the path in front of her, she could push her grief back down her throat and into her chest. It made the space around her heart ache but at least she could concentrate on what she was doing. One painful step at a time, she made some progress on her journey. Sometimes she would let her guard down and then a sliver of sharp grief would escape from her chest. It would slice at her throat and she would stumble and fall again, the tears soaking into the rock under her cheek. Eventually she managed to control even this pain. Numbness was better than grief. Numbness meant she could put one foot in front of the other.

Days passed. Melissa walked through the world without really seeing it, knowing that eventually something would happen: it always did. There was always a place to go, a house to find, or a lesson to learn. If she just kept moving, she knew that she would end up somewhere. At this point she didn't care where that somewhere was, as long as it was different to where she had been. Melissa thought a lot about her home, and would spend hours of every day imagining the rooms she lived in down to the finest detail. She had left a glass of water on her bedside table, and imagined that it had probably dried out by now. Melissa wondered if someone had turned off her alarm clock or if it was still going off for five minutes at six o'clock every morning.

When she had imagined her apartment in fine detail she turned her attention to her office, and then to her gym. Running out of places to think about she began remembering the rooms of her childhood home again. The pattern on the wallpaper that had been in the dining room eluded her. She thought it had been green, but she couldn't remember. She could remember that at the door between the dining room and the kitchen there had been a patch of carpet that was really rough under her bare feet. Her mother had dropped a whole roast chicken on the floor there once and no matter how many times her mother had cleaned the carpet, it had never been soft again. Melissa could remember running her bare toes along the edge of the stain and feeling the carpet scratching her feet. It was funny that she could remember the stain and not the pattern on the walls.

It was early one evening when Melissa realized that she wasn't getting anywhere. She had been walking for days yet nothing seemed to change. Sitting with her back against a rock, she watched the flames dancing in the small fire she had made for company. Around her, rocks, stones, scruffy trees, bushes and her never ending path were all that she could see. The horizon was unchanged. Every day she was moving, but she wasn't getting anywhere. A deep breath turned into a yawn. Shifting her weight forward she gazed looked into the flames.

"I don't know what to do next," she murmured to the fire. She waited, half expecting an answer this time. None came.

The next morning started in much the same way her mornings had for a long time. Melissa opened her eyes and looked at the misty dawn sky above her. For the briefest moment she forgot everything except being awake and then she remembered and the weight of her pain threatened to drown her alive. Taking a deep breath, she swallowed several times and felt the numbness return. She knew that eventually the mornings would begin with numb and she wouldn't have to worry anymore about waking up. It would happen. It just took time.

It wasn't until she had climbed her third hill of the day that she realized that this time something was different. As she reached the top she could see her path ahead leading back down into a stony, brown valley. In this valley, however, she was surprised to see something glinting at her in the distance. After so many days of seeing nothing but grey and brown rocks and shrubs, her heart leapt in anticipation of something else being there and she quickened her pace until she was almost running down the hill.

Soon a building came into focus. As she got closer she could see that it was a window that had been cheerfully winking at her in the sun. The windows stretched across the front of a long, low building that looked like a roadside restaurant. The walls were covered in thick white plaster that had been stained brown in places by the dust and the wind. Squared off on the top, the roof was shingled in brownish-red tiles. From the outside, you couldn't tell what sort of place it was. The curtains were drawn, and there were no signs of life anywhere.

Melissa couldn't decide whether or not to go in. Looking down at her feet for an answer, she found none. Her path had disappeared in the dust, and her feet were brown with filth. Studying the building, she reasoned that her path had been lead-ing her in the same direction for days. She could either keep going as she was and hope that something would change or she could take a chance and see what was behind the door. The dust of the journey filled her nose, and felt like sandpaper between her teeth. Tired and thirsty, the only thing holding her back was the feeling that she wasn't up to another lesson. Her heart and her feet ached equally. In the end her feet won out over her head. Something had to change, so this might as well be it.

A bell tinkled merrily as she pushed open the door. A wave of sweet, clean, cool air brushed her cheeks and she greedily sucked it into her lungs. The door closed behind her with another tinkle of the bell, but no one took any notice. The walls were painted deep, rich yellow and were dotted with mirrors and menus written in white chalk on black boards. The chairs, tables and other furniture were all painted black and every flat surface held a vase holding a single red flower. The whole room felt very chic and glamorous. Melissa smoothed her hands over her dirty clothes in embarrassment.

"Hello," a woman appeared at her side, making Melissa jump. People were always doing that here. "Welcome. You must be tired, can I show you to a table?" Melissa swallowed the dust in her throat and nodded.

The woman moved gracefully through the room, moving her hips to avoid hitting the many chairs that held her guests. Dressed all in black, she wore a tight fitting long-sleeved back top, cropped trousers and black ballet flats. Her hair was cut in a chic bob and she wore it tucked behind her ears. She turned and smiled at Melissa as she found a table for one.

"Is this okay?"

"Yes, thank you," Melissa managed to say. Her voice felt strange in her throat and sounded scratched from lack of use. "I am afraid I haven't got any money," she started.

"Oh, that's okay," the woman smiled. "We aren't that kind of place."

"What kind of place are you?" Melissa asked, puzzled. The other diners were all sipping from glasses and nibbling from plates. It looked like a restaurant to her.

"I guess you could say we are a kind of resting place – a waiting room if you will – for those on long journeys," the woman smiled again. "Now, what can I bring you? You look like you have come from a long way. A drink?" She looked at Melissa thoughtfully. "How about I bring you something to quench that thirst?" Melissa nodded gratefully.

In just a few moments, the woman was back. "I am Delia," she said, putting a tall glass and a menu in front of Melissa. "Now, have a drink, think about what you want, and I will be back in a few minutes."

Tall and slim and covered with a thin film of ice, the glass made a wet circle on the black table. Melissa noticed this before she noticed that the drink was soft pink in colour, or that a fat strawberry had been sliced so that it sat on the rim of the glass. When she did notice it, all she saw was salvation. Carefully taking the strawberry from the glass, she held it in one of her hands. With the other she raised the glass to her lips. It smelled faintly of peaches and she could feel it flowing all of the way down to her stomach, soothing the soreness as it went. When the glass was empty she put it back down on the table and licked her lips. Running the back of her hand over her mouth she could feel the icy moisture left there. The strawberry was ripe and juicy but she wasn't ready for it yet. Carefully returning it to the rim of her glass, she opened the menu.

"Have you decided what you would like to have?" Delia smiled, placing a tiny plate on the table. Taking the strawberry from Melissa's glass, she put it on the plate and picked up the glass, holding it in one hand as she stood waiting.

"I haven't really thought," Melissa started. "What was she hungry for? She thought of Mary and smiled. Melissa poked at the strawberry with one finger and thought about what she wanted to eat.

"I'd love a pot of green tea please," she said. "And I'd like some nice bread and a small dish of olives."

"Coming right up," Delia smiled, leaving her alone.

As she was waiting for Delia, Melissa finally took a good look around her at the other diners. Women of every colour and every age were sipping drinks and nibbling on delicacies at most of the other tables. A woman wearing a beautiful red dress sat at the next table. Feeling nosy, Melissa looked down at the woman's feet to see what shoes she was wearing and nearly fell out of her chair with surprise. From the waist down the woman was completely embedded in her chair. Carved wooden vines curled around her legs and held her securely in place. She appeared unconcerned, continuing to sip her tea and to laugh gaily with the woman who sat next to her.

Wondering if it was just this woman in particular, Melissa looked around her more carefully. Sure enough, many of the women were completely stuck to their chairs. There were others whose chairs had only just begun to take them over, and a few who didn't seem to have any problem getting up. Standing for a moment, Melissa looked at the seat of her own chair. It looked solid enough. She sat down gingerly, poised to leap from her seat if she felt any change.

"Here we are, some tea, olives, and bread. Can I get you anything else?" Delia smiled, placing each item on the table as she said its name.

"Delia, what's all this about? Why are those women stuck to their chairs?" Melissa hissed, acutely aware of the seat beneath her.

"Oh, some of them have been here a really long time," Delia answered.

"Why? What is here that makes them get stuck like that?" Melissa asked.

"Oh, it's not what's here," Delia said, shaking her head. "It's what's next." Melissa twisted to look straight at Delia.

"What do you mean? What's next?"

"The only way out of here is through that door," Delia smiled gently, pointing across the room at a large wooden door. Melissa wrinkled her forehead in confusion.

"I don't understand. What's through there that is so scary?" Melissa asked.

"Go over and have a listen for yourself," Delia said. "I'll keep you topped up with tea, shall I? Can I get you anything else?" When Melissa shook her head, Delia moved off to another table.

Melissa sat for a few minutes and watched the door on the other side of the room. No one went near it, nobody came through it and no one even looked at it. It was tall and made of dark brown wood. Once it had been highly polished, but the place on the door where you would put your hand to open it was mottled with hand and fingerprints. She got up slowly and walked curiously across the room. When she reached the door she realized that much of the conversation in the room had quieted. Everyone was watching her.

"It's just a door," she whispered to herself. Reaching out and touching the wood with her fingertips she found it was smooth and warm to the touch. She flattened her hands against it, but didn't push. Melissa heard a collective intake of breath behind her, and knew that they were all waiting for her to do something. She turned and looked back into the room. Nervously they all turned back to their conversations, pretending that they hadn't been watching. Turning again, Melissa pondered the door.

Stepping closer, she rested her head against the wood, listening like she used to do at doors when she was a child. Closing her eyes, she tuned out the room.

The wood under her ear was warm and felt like it was pulsing. The sound coming from beyond the door but it was a sound unlike any other she had heard before, her skin tingled down to her toes in instinctive fear. Though the sound was hollow and muffled, she could hear someone screaming a long, drawn out, agonizing scream. It was an unmistakable sound of suffering. Was that right? Was that what she was hearing? Melissa knew that on this journey, things had not always been what they had seemed, so she took a deep breath and opened the door a tiny crack, trying to peer inside. Darkness and the sounds of suffering swirled out, nearly overwhelming her. Stumbling backwards in her haste to get away, she let the door close again. Head down in shame and confusion, she rushed back to her table. With sweaty palms she reached for her tea, the cup rattling in the saucer as she held it.

"You okay honey?" Delia was standing beside the table, watching her shakily sipping at her tea.

"No. What is that place?" Melissa answered, looking up with angry eyes. She was surprised to find that she was not afraid. Instead, she was furious.

"It's the Wailing Room," Delia said, pulling out the chair across from Melissa and sitting down.

"The what?" Melissa exclaimed angrily.

"People only arrive here when they are beginning to dry up," Delia explained. "You arrived because you weren't going to get anywhere on the path you were on."

"I was getting somewhere!" Melissa protested.

"That's not what I mean. People arrive here when their bodies begin to get stuck. Your body needs to clear out some stuff," Delia smiled.

"You want to run that by me again?" Melissa said, raising one eyebrow.

"Sometimes what the journey gives us is too much to bear and we begin swallowing it down instead of letting it out. The more pain and suffering we hold inside of our bodies the less room there is for anything else to flourish."

"I don't get it. Sadness isn't a physical thing, it's a feeling," Melissa protested.

"Well that would be true if your body and your mind were separate things, but they are not. When something happens that is too much for your mind to cope with, it files it away somewhere in your anatomy. Those things aren't supposed to be there so eventually your body has to remind your brain that it needs its space back," Delia smiled, helping herself to an olive. Melissa's face showed her disgust at Delia's explanation.

"Oh, give me a break," Melissa snorted. "So I have a bad back because I was mad at my mother when I was a kid?"

"No, actually, your back is where you tend to store money worries. Mother issues take up a whole other part of your body."

"Are you kidding me?" Melissa raged.

"No. Tell me the truth. When you last felt really sad, did you let yourself grieve? Did you let yourself fall apart and cry and wail and scream until you felt better?"

"No," Melissa shook her head. "I didn't have time to do that. If I had started crying that way, I might never have stopped. I had things to do so I got on and did them."

"So how do you feel now about that sadness? How does your chest feel when you think about it?" Delia popped another olive into her mouth.

"Tight," Melissa admitted.

"Throat hurt?" Delia asked, wiping a bit of olive oil from her chin with her hand. Melissa nodded, her anger draining away.

"It's stuck. It's stuck and you are carrying it around. You are carrying it around on top of all of the other pain that you have not let yourself feel, like a great big elephant in your body."

"But if I let myself feel all of my pain, I might never stop crying again. Delia, if I let myself feel all the pain that is there I will die." Melissa nearly choked on her words as she said them. Tears filled her throat and her eyes, but she furiously blinked them away. She swallowed several times, but her throat was thick and tight.

"Melissa, if you continue to hold all of your pain inside your body, you will die," Delia said toughly. "You need to free your body up to feel all of the other feelings too. By stopping one, you will just numb yourself to all of them."

"But I have cried before and it hasn't made the pain go away. I have been sad all over again the next day," Melissa argued.

"Then you need to grieve all over again the next day," Delia shrugged. "If that's what it takes. Eventually you will be able to be sad or angry or to miss someone without it feeling like your heart is about to shatter. And eventually you won't mind so much because you will have also freed yourself to remember and feel the good stuff too."

Melissa didn't know what else to say. She knew now why there were so many women here stuck to their seats. To leave here and get on with her journey she would have to feel again but she wasn't ready. She wondered if she ever would be.

With a final stolen olive in her mouth Delia stood up and turned to serve another table, leaving Melissa to her own thoughts. She took a sip of her tea. The liquid had cooled while they were talking and it felt strange on her tongue. Topping it up with some tea from the pot and holding her cup in both hands, she raised it to her mouth but didn't drink. There was too much to think about.

"Fresh pot?" Delia smiled, shaking Melissa out of her reverie. Startled to find that her tea was cold all over again, she smiled and let Delia take her cold tea away and replace it with a hot one. She picked up a piece of bread and dipped it in the oil that pooled around the olives. Raising it to her mouth she realized that she had not eaten properly in several days. Chewing the bread slowly, she enjoyed the fragrance of the olive oil and yeast combined with the scent of her tea. Sighing, she felt her shoulders relax for the first time in a long time just before Delia appeared beside her again.

"I'm really hungry," Melissa said. "Will you bring me something more robust to eat?"

"Of course," Delia smiled. "What would you like?"

"Some fish, I think," Melissa nodded to herself. "And some vegetables? And a little bit more bread."

"No problem," Delia said, clearing away Melissa's empty breadbasket. She was back a few minutes later with a steaming hot plate of food and some cutlery rolled up in a red napkin. Disappearing again, she soon came back with a refilled breadbasket and a small pot each of salt and black pepper.

"Can I get you anything else?" Delia asked. When Melissa shook her head, Delia left her alone to eat. Melissa unrolled her napkin, catching the cutlery and putting it on the table, and spreading the napkin on her lap. Even though she was very hungry, she was determined to eat slowly and enjoy this meal. Unclear on what to do next, she could see that other women were getting more and more entangled in their seats. Wiggling in her own chair, she realized that it already felt different. Looking down, she saw that it was beginning to form around her shape and she realized how easy it would be to stay stuck in this place. Numbness was definitely an easier option than pain.

When she had eaten her fill, she pushed her plate away. Delia came and quietly removed it, sensing that Melissa's thoughts were somewhere else. Melissa was thinking back on her journey. She wondered if Lola and Natalie had started their journey yet. Were Emma and Grace still sitting at that table or were they just behind her on their own paths? Then there was Elle, who had wanted to protect her. She remembered how much Elle had helped her at the beginning and she also thought about how she had stopped needing any help by the time they had reached that bridge.

Deep in her heart Melissa knew that she had learned some valuable lessons so far, and that they might only get harder to learn, but sooner or later she was going to have to continue on her path. It could be now or it could be later, but it was going to happen. Her only decision in the matter was when. The darkness and the pain that she had experienced earlier that day had frightened her, but she knew that the door held the key to getting home. She could wait three months to 'get it' like she had at the cottage, or she could have three tries at it like she had in the garden, or she could just get up and move through the door and deal with whatever was on the other side. She would never be braver or stronger or more ready than she was right now, and the longer she waited, the more frightened and stuck she would become.

Melissa scanned the table in front of her, picked up the strawberry from the plate and bit into it. Biting off the stem, she took the rest of the berry into her mouth and rolled the flesh around on her tongue. It was sticky and sharp and sweet all at once, and tasted of fresh air and sunny days. She swallowed and wiped her mouth with her napkin. With a little difficulty she got up from her chair and her napkin fell to the floor unnoticed. Bending, she picked her bag up and pulled it onto her shoulders.

With a deep, shuddering breath full of nerves and panic, she took one step towards the door. The conversations around her stopped again. All eyes were on her.

"It's just a door," she whispered to herself again. Head held high, she walked through the mottle of chairs and bodies to the door. This time she didn't look back. Heart pounding, she put her hand flat on the surface of the door again. It was warm and soft and vibrated gently under her skin. The scent of the red blossoms in the room filled her as opened the door and stepped through.

Chapter Twelve

I t was only after the door had closed behind her that she realized she was squeezing her eyes shut and holding her breath. Even after she understood this she paused for a moment before she moved. She couldn't feel anything. She couldn't smell anything. She couldn't hear anything. There was no feeling of dread or pain or shame or bleakness as there had been when she had opened the door the last time. Slowly she exhaled, relaxing her shoulders. When nothing happened, she cautiously opened one eye. Then her mouth fell open in amazement as she opened the other eye.

She was not standing in some horrible dark nightmare of a place; she was standing in someone's living room. It was decorated in soft beige and white and shades of brown. A deep, inviting couch sat opposite a huge dark brown recliner. There were tables at either end of the couch, beside the chair and in the centre of the room. Each table held a box of tissues and a glass of water. Suspiciously, she dropped her bag on the floor and walked around the room. The walls were painted in soft cream and had pretty pictures of meadows and fields and sea towns on them. She was confused. This was the Wailing Room? She had expected something far more sinister.

Feeling uncomfortable she sat down on one end of the couch. It was soft and supported her perfectly. Apart from the door she had come through there were no doors or windows. She waited, not knowing what to do and assuming that someone would come and give her some instructions.

"What's next then?" she whispered. The sound of her voice sounded strange in the still air. She took a deep breath and then exhaled, feeling her shoulders drop down and her neck soften. She sat further back on the couch, resting her head against the high back. Breathing deeply again she realized that she was clenching her jaw. Tilting her head back she opened her mouth wide. Working her jaw in small circles she could feel the tension leaving her face. When she felt her face muscles relax she took another deep breath, all the while expecting something strange to happen. This whole journey had been so weird that she wondered where she would find herself in a moment, but nothing happened.

"Go on, what's next?" Melissa said, whispering a little bit louder and sitting up straight again. The minutes ticked by. She had become pretty good at waiting, but it was a lot easier when you knew what you were waiting for. Wiggling her feet and looking around, she stuck her bottom lip out as she concentrated on the ceiling. An itch drew her attention to her collarbone. Moving her head around she realized that her throat hurt a little. Cupping her neck with her hand, she massaged the muscles carefully.

"Hello!" she called out. This time her voice was loud in the small room. She smiled, feeling strangely bold for making so much noise. Her hand was still resting on her throat, and she liked feeling the muscles along her neck tense when she spoke.

"My name is Melissa," she almost shouted, exhilarating in the sound and the feeling. "Is anyone else here?" If this was supposed to be the Wailing Room, she was confused. What was she supposed to be doing? She thought about her journey again. Was she sad? She had felt that way when she was talking to Delia. She had not dealt with the sadness of Elle's death, but she also knew that there was far more sadness underneath that pain. Maybe she should try to let it out. Maybe she should let herself cry. Maybe then she could move on.

Feeling the couch holding her body, Melissa tried to relax. Knowing that her grief went far far deeper than losing Elle, she tried to think of all of the reasons for her pain. Grief from old losses and old disappointments was lodged somewhere inside and she knew it. Closing her eyes, she focused on the sad, tight place under her heart, thinking that surely that was where it all had gone. Her grandmother's face appeared, and then the faces of two special men who had caused her heart to break. Melissa saw her parents, feeling the depth of what she believed was their disappointment in her, and felt the crushing agony of her own as yet unrealized dream of a true love and two curly-haired children. All of what she thought she was supposed to be doing and what she regretted began to eat its way through the walls she had built to protect herself. Then, something inside of her shifted. Remembering the clutching sharpness of grief, Melissa's eyes opened. Becoming frantic, she sat up, swallowing down any pain that she had begun to feel.

"Hello?" Melissa said a little louder again. This time the word caught in her throat and she coughed, trying to dislodge it. It felt like she had taken a vitamin pill and it had got stuck half way down. Swallowing several times, she coughed again, trying to dislodge whatever it was that was sticking to her. It shifted a little, but she started to panic when she realized that it was moving up instead of down.

Melissa shivered and the small motion sent tingles through her body. She rested her head against the back of the couch again and took a very deep breath. As she exhaled, she gently wrapped her hand around her throat. For a moment she sat quietly before she realized that there was more for her to breathe out. She did, allowing her shoulders to drop even more.

A sliver of a cry escaped from her throat. It was a tiny, mournful sound, not much louder than a sigh. Silent tears began to flow over her cheeks. A moment later the tears turned to quiet sobs. Memories flooded her. Faces and places from her childhood swam through her tears, but for the first time she didn't chase them away. As she greeted each one she could feel a different part of her body changing. Sometimes there was pain and sometimes there was an ache, but all of the memories left her with a deeper ability to breathe. She let the tears and sobs fall where they wanted to fall, giving herself the space to sit in the middle of it all and cry.

When her tears had finally dried, she took a deep breath. At the top of the breath, her whole body shivered. Goosebumps covered her skin. She felt light-headed and a little dizzy, as if she had been holding her breath for years and her body did not know what to do with all of the fresh oxygen. She closed her eyes and held the breath for a moment and then she opened her eyes and exhaled. To her surprise, her breath came out in a crisp, white cloud. The mist swirled crisply in front of her face for a moment and then melted in the warm air.

"What was that?" She whispered to the room. There was no answer.

Melissa opened her eyes. There was something soft under her cheek, and she remembered that she had curled up on one of the couches to wait for what would happen next. Yawning and stretching, she didn't sit up immediately. The couch was very comfortable and the room was quite dark. Her body felt strange: stiff and sore, and yet light and very relaxed.

The soft scrape of a door opening made her sit up.

"Hi there," Delia smiled, holding a tray. "How are you feeling?"

"I'm not sure," Melissa answered honestly. "I don't remember ever feeling like this before, so I am not sure what to call it."

"That's pretty normal," Delia said, putting the tray down on the coffee table. "I thought you might like some breakfast. Have lots of honey, it soothes the throat."

"Thank you," Melissa smiled, realizing that she was quite hungry. She had no idea how long she had been in the room, and her body felt so foreign to her, she wanted to feed it to see how it would feel. The tray held a pot of tea, some fruit and some toast and honey. Looking up to smile her thanks to Delia, she found she was alone.

Melissa ate her fill of the toast and honey and fresh, ripe berries before she poured herself a cup of tea. It was fresh with the fragrance of mint and she sighed as she held the cup in both of her hands. In between sips, she would occasionally reach forward and pop a blueberry into her mouth. She didn't know what was coming next, but she knew that she felt better than she had in a very long time.

The remains of Melissa's tea had long gone cold in the pot when she finally got up from the couch. Stretching and wandering around the room, wondering what she was supposed to do next. Surely what had just happened to her was the lesson that she was meant to learn.

"So am I done?" She asked the empty room. "Have I learned my lesson? Can I go home now?" No matter what she did, she could not seem to settle down. She even opened her bag to see if there was something that she needed, but nothing new sat waiting for her.

"Delia?" Melissa called as loudly as she could, but there was no answer. Finally, frustrated by the situation she decided to go and find Delia. At least then she would have someone to talk to. Her persistent knocking on the door got no answer.

"Well obviously they aren't going to answer the door if they think that there is screaming and wailing going on on the other side," she said aloud to herself. "I wouldn't either. But maybe if I just go back through and tell them that it isn't scary, then I will be able to leave and get back on the path."

Melissa nodded to herself happily, feeling more in control of the situation now. As she passed the table to get her bag, she noticed that there was a note attached to the jar of honey that she hadn't noticed before.

"Honey is good for a sore throat. Take the jar with our compliments." Melissa put her hand to her throat. Was her throat sore? It no longer felt sore but she wondered whether it might be in the future. Squeezing the lid on as tightly as it would go she tucked the jar of honey into her knapsack. With one last look around at the comfortable room, she pulled at the big wooden door.

Chapter Thirteen

The door opened easily. The now-familiar feeling of the world spinning and the bottom dropping out of her stomach hit her and she paused just past the threshold. Dazed, she took a step forward and then stumbled backwards in alarm as a car screeched across her path. She turned to go back through the door but all that stood behind her was a solid concrete wall. In terror, Melissa pressed herself back against the cold stone. She was in a city! It had been so long since she had been in the city that she began to panic. Breathing carefully, she fought to calm her heartbeat.

"I can do this," she whispered to herself. Then it dawned on her that she could be back in her own city. Her head shot up as she scanned her surroundings wondering if she was home.

The street she was on did not look familiar so she searched for a street sign or an address somewhere, but could not see anything. Slowly and carefully she pushed away from the wall. To her right she could see a street leading her towards an intersection. To her left an alley receded into darkness. The car that had frightened her so much had come out of the alley. Turning right, she headed down the street.

Nothing was familiar and yet everything was. She could have been on any street in any city. There were bus shelters with posters in them and buildings stretching up towards the sky. Leaves and bits of garbage filled the gutters, and all around her was the strange city smell of dust and fuel and people and stone. She glanced in a few shop windows as she passed, but was too intent on finding her way to pay very much attention to the contents. Once she knew where she was she would slow down but for now she needed a sign and she needed it as soon as possible. Panic began to sting at the back of her throat.

At the edge of the intersection, she stopped. Shielding her eyes, she searched for an answer, but nothing made sense. There were no street signs here that would help her so she decided that she needed to find a person. There were a few waiting across the street for the lights to change, but she didn't want to waste any more time. Turning to look back down the street behind her she saw a woman waiting under the bus shelter. With a cold flutter of relief, Melissa walked back the way she'd come. The woman was watching the road and kept checking her watch impatiently. Melissa understood that she needed to make this quick.

"Excuse me," Melissa said firmly as she stepped under the sheltering roof. "I wonder if you could help me. I'm not sure where I am and..." Melissa's words trailed off as the woman turned to face her. Bile filled Melissa's throat as terror and revulsion froze her to the spot. The woman looked at Melissa impatiently. Melissa's mouth hung open in a soft gasp of confusion as she tried to understand what it was that she was seeing. The face and head of the woman in front of her were quite normal, but where her neck should have been there was just shadow and space. Below that space the woman's body was wizened and shrivelled. Melissa could see her bones sticking through under her clothes, and anywhere skin was visible it looked like hard, dried leather. Melissa's own skin prickled with danger.

"What is it you want?" The woman asked.

"Oh, it's nothing. I'm sorry to bother you," Melissa whispered, whirling around and walking back up the street towards the intersection. Keeping her head down, she studied the ground as she tried to get her heart to start beating normally again. She remembered the women back at Mary's restaurant. Was it possible that this woman had just come from there? But then she remembered that she wasn't wearing Mary's glasses, and the woman hadn't had the energy trails above her head. In fact, her head hadn't even been attached to her body.

Melissa walked with her own head down for several blocks. When she had regained her composure she remembered that she still didn't know where she was going. Slowly raising her head, she looked around. The streets had become busier in the last few minutes and there were people rushing everywhere. The longer she stood still, the more people bumped into her. Feeling frightened and small, she pushed through the crowds and stood against the nearest building, dropping her bag at her feet so that she could feel the wall against her back. Reassuringly cold and solid, the stone made her feel grounded again. Flattening herself tightly against the building, she clutched at it with her fingertips and enjoyed the soft scrape of the stone against her skin. Feeling like she was on solid ground once again, Melissa made herself have a good look around.

"It must be after five o'clock," Melissa murmured. She knew how a city felt when five o'clock came. She knew how these people felt. In fact, she could feel it all around her. It felt of relief mixed with fatigue and resignation. No matter how they felt about going home, tomorrow they would just have to do it all over again. Melissa shivered and pressed herself harder against the wall. The steady hum of traffic, the sharp blaring of horns and the shuffle of uncountable feet were the unmistakable sounds of a city going about its business. But there were other sounds layered in amongst those voices. These ones weren't coming from the world around her, these were coming from the people as they walked past. As each person moved near her, Melissa could hear a dry rattle that sounded as if their bones were clunking against each other. The sound made Melissa's teeth ache in their sockets. This sound was bad enough, but there was another sound that came with it. Melissa could sense rather than properly hear a deep mournful cry coming from each person. It was as if deep in each person's core they were screaming. Melissa's knees buckled under her and she slid to sit on the cold cement.

Scanning the street, she searched for some answers or some hope. Across the street in front of her was a shop window. This at least was familiar. As she looked, she noticed that the mannequins were all dressed in white dresses. Printed across their fronts were the words, 'You aren't good enough.' Swallowing her revulsion, Melissa looked at a different window. This one was full of furniture. Across the awning a banner hung, emblazoned with the same words. In another window, there were female mannequins suspended above the floor on wires. They had no feet and no hands and no necks. 'You aren't good enough' screamed at her from every window and every sign. 'Not good enough, not good enough, not good enough,' echoed through her head.

The longer she sat still and waited for something to happen, the harder it was to get up and move again. Even the air felt like it was trying to smother her. Melissa moved so that the back of her head was resting against the wall, and it was then that she saw her. A woman in a blue coat moved across Melissa's field of vision. Sensing that there was something different about her, Melissa kept watching. The woman reached into her pocket for something and when she brought her hand out, a piece of paper fell to the ground. Stooping to pick it up, she half-turned towards Melissa and Melissa realized that this woman was whole. Her head and her body were connected to each other, her bones had flesh on them and her body wasn't rattling or crying.

Melissa didn't know what she was going to do next, but she knew that she had to find out why this woman was different. Scrambling to her feet, she grabbed her bag and ran through the crowd, hoping to keep the blue coat in sight. Frantic, she even pushed a few people aside in her desperation. Melissa had just about reached her when the woman stepped onto a bus. As Melissa reached the curb, the bus pulled away, leaving Melissa to watch the woman find her seat through the windows as the bus drove down the street.

Hours went by and Melissa's hope began to waver. After losing the woman, Melissa had begun to pay more attention to the people walking by. Every now and then Melissa would glimpse someone like the woman in the blue coat. She couldn't figure out what it was about them that made them different, but each time she saw one and tried to follow them, they slipped away from her. Wondering whether she should give up, Melissa sat dejectedly on the front step of one of the buildings.

A bus stop stood between her and the street. Glancing towards it, Melissa caught sight of her reflection in the glass. With small cry, she reached up and touched her neck. Her reflection showed a healthy, normal head, but to her horror, her neck was missing. A look at her hands confirmed it: they were dry and brittle, and the bones rattled around under the slack bag of skin holding them together.

A flicker of bright red caught her eye. A woman was crossing the street in front of her and Melissa watched her closely, wondering what had caught her attention. As the woman moved, her coat flapped around her legs, showing glimpses of a bright red lining underneath. As the woman moved closer, Melissa realized that this was another one of the women who were different from the others. This woman's head was firmly attached to her body. This woman's bones didn't rattle when she walked. This woman was not crying from her core.

Melissa stood up and moved so that she was in step with the woman. Determined not to lose this one, Melissa followed her as closely as she dared. What was it that was different about her? Melissa trotted along behind her, standing outside as the woman went into a bakery. As far as Melissa could see there was nothing unusual about her. She bought normal things, thanked the person behind the counter, and carried her shopping bags in one hand while she fished a list out of her pocket with the other. She walked normally, she talked normally and she looked like any other woman in any other city going about her daily business, but here in this strange world, the difference was that this woman's eyes sparkled and snapped with life. There was something ripe and full about her. Melissa couldn't see through to her bones because there was flesh and blood in the way. There was more to her than the others.

"Thank you," Melissa heard the woman call behind her as she came out of a florist cradling a package wrapped in brown paper in her arms. Melissa stayed several feet behind her as they turned off the main road and onto a street that was more residential. The woman's pace quickened and Melissa wondered if she knew that she was being followed. The woman turned and walked towards a house with a large gold 25 on the door. Rather than going up the stairs, she opened a small gate beside the house and went down a small set of steps.

"Well now what?" Melissa asked no one in particular. Sitting down on the steps that led to the front door of number 25 she rested her chin in her palm and wondered what she should do next. She couldn't spend the night on these steps waiting for the woman to come out again.

"Are you waiting for someone?" A voice interrupted Melissa's thoughts. Melissa jumped up from the steps and turned around. A woman stood in the doorway, holding the door partially open with one hand. Melissa had to swallow several times before she was able to answer. This was not the woman she had been following. The space between this woman's head and her body was thick with shadows and the hand that held the door was weathered and clawed. Melissa forced herself to smile.

"Um, yes. I was just waiting for your downstairs neighbour to get home," Melissa lied.

"Tera? I think I heard her come in a few minutes ago," the woman said, moving forward a little. Melissa heard the rattling of bones under skin, and swayed a little from the cry that was swirling around them both.

"Oh, thank you," Melissa said. "I'll just go for a walk around the block and let her get settled. Maybe she was busy when I knocked before." She stepped back and turned onto the sidewalk, unable to get away fast enough. Walking further down the street, she looked back to make sure that the woman was gone. Melissa wandered up and down the street a few times, rolling the day over and over in her head as she kept close enough to watch Tera's gate and far enough away that the woman would not come out and talk to her again.

It was beginning to get dark. Melissa sat on the steps of a house across the street from number 25 and thought about what to do. There was a chill in the air and the sounds of the city began to swirl around her again. Curling her arms around her legs, she tried to warm herself as she watched the house. She could just see the tops of Tera's windows. The lights were on and the windows glowed faintly yellow against the dark walls above.

"What do I do now?" Melissa whispered, plunking her bag on the step beside her. Reaching inside the bag, she took out her grey sweater. Before putting it on, she held it in her hands for a few minutes. Feeling the soft wool against her fingers, she stared at the pattern the stitches made and let the questions fill her. What was she doing sitting here on a step in the dark in a strange city? What was she doing being afraid? Everything else that she had done up until now had had some meaning, why was she expecting this to be any different? Why was she expecting this place to follow the old rules when she clearly had been living by a different set on this journey? What was she waiting for?

Putting the sweater back into her bag, Melissa stood up. Brushing herself off, she put her bag back on her shoulders. Standing up a little straighter she took a deep breath, looked both ways and crossed the street. Letting herself in the little gate, Melissa descended a small set of steps and stood in front of Tera's front door. It was a small door, created to fit into the space under the stairs of the house above. The door was painted deep green and on the door was a silver sign that read 25 ½. Melissa smiled despite her nerves. Summoning up all of her courage, Melissa reached out and knocked on the door.

Chapter Fourteen

For a long moment, Melissa thought that there would be no answer. She almost turned to peek in the windows, but then the door opened. Melissa realized with horror that she had not thought of any explanation for her presence. The woman with the red coat stood before her smiling quizzically and Melissa's mind went completely blank.

"Hello," the woman smiled. "Can I help you?"

"I hope so," Melissa managed. "But I am not sure what it is you can help me with."

"Do you want to come in?" The woman's smile was wide and warm and trusting. Melissa knew that somewhere in that smile were the answers she was looking for.

"Yes, please," Melissa smiled. The woman pushed the door open a little wider and Melissa gratefully stepped through into a small hallway.

"I'm Tera," the woman smiled again, closing the door behind them.

"I'm Melissa."

"I'm very pleased to meet you Melissa," Tera said. "You look like you could use a cup of tea." Melissa smiled with gratitude. Tera showed her through a door and into a snug living room. "Please, have a seat. What kind of tea would you like? I have just about everything you can think of," Tera laughed. "In fact, I think I have a bit of a tea addiction!"

"Oh, I don't know," Melissa smiled. "Just bring me whatever you are having." Tera cocked her head to one side and studied Melissa carefully.

"Do you like cinnamon?" Tera asked. When Melissa nodded, Tera smiled. "Then I have just the thing," she smiled, disappearing into another room.

Melissa dropped her bag onto the floor and sunk gratefully onto the soft couch. The walls were painted deep, rich red, and furniture was an eclectic mix of colours and fabrics. There were no lights on the ceiling, so all of the light was provided by small table lamps. Half of the shelves were full of candles and bowls and sculptures of animals, and the other half were filled with a tumble of books. The result was a cozy, warm room that made her feel completely comfortable for the first time in a very long time.

"Please, make yourself at home," Tera called from the kitchen. Melissa could see that the kitchen was decorated quite differently from this room. The walls were white and she could see a dark brown dining table with a big green plant on it, and benches instead of chairs. She couldn't see the counter. Bending over, she took off her shoes. As she was pulling her them over her toes, the dry bones rattled together in protest. Her feet were as empty as the rest of her.

"Are you hungry?" Tera asked, coming in and putting a tray down in front of Melissa. Melissa realized that she was famished.

"Well, I've got some things here that you can nibble on," Tara said kindly, leaning forward to pour the tea out of a beautiful teapot. It was blue and had butterflies all over it. Tera put the pot down and leaned toward Melissa, offering her tea in a pretty polka dotted pink cup.

"Thank you," Melissa said honestly. There was a basket of scones and rolls, some soft cheese, and pots of jam and honey. Melissa gratefully took a scone and spread it with jam. With a sigh of pleasure she took a bite and sat back on the couch.

"So, tell me about yourself," Tera said, helping herself to a scone and spreading it with strawberry jam. Melissa took a sip of the hot tea. It was heavily spiced and warmed her as it went down.

"I don't know what to tell you," Melissa said. "In my other life I would have told you what I did and who I was with, but none of that makes sense here."

"Oh, I am so glad to hear that!" Tera exclaimed. "I never really want to talk about that stuff anyway. Tell me why it doesn't make sense."

"Well, I have been on the strangest adventure," Melissa began. Tera sat back with her scone in her hand and focused her gaze on Melissa. Encouraged, Melissa began to tell Tera about her journey. Every now and then Tera would interrupt with a question or would fill her teacup, but for the most part she just listened. When Melissa got up to this morning, she stopped.

"So how did you get to my front door?" Tera laughed when Melissa was clearly pausing in discomfort.

"I followed you," Melissa answered.

"Me? Why?" Tera asked, sipping her tea.

"Because you were different from everyone else," Melissa admitted, feeling like she had nothing to lose.

"How?" Tera asked.

"Can't you see that the other people here are different from you?" Melissa asked, pausing for a bite of her scone. Tera thought about that for a moment.

"No, not really. I know I have felt different for a long time, but I could never really see it."

"Well, you are," Melissa said. "To my eyes, most of the people here don't have heads connected to their body."

"Oh, that!" Tera said, throwing back her head in laughter. "I know about that."

"But I thought," Melissa began.

"Oh, no, no, no," Tera stopped her. "I can't see that, but I know it is there. I think that most of the people you meet every day have dried up."

"Not completely," Melissa said. "Their heads seem to be the only part of them that is normal."

"That's because their heads are the only part getting any blood!" Tera laughed.

"What?" Melissa nearly chocked on a bite of scone.

"Well, it stands to reason," Tera began. "Most people around here are only living in their heads. They spend all of their time worrying and being afraid and comparing themselves and their lives to other people. Most of the people around here believe the garbage that advertising spits out. Most people are terrified that they are not good enough as they are. They have completely forgotten to live from their whole body, because they have dis-connected with it," Tera's eyes were flashing.

"Disconnected?" Melissa asked, sitting forward.

"Yeah. When people get too wrapped up in fear and anger and guilt and worry, they are just living from their head. They are living from their intellect and ignoring their instinct. Instinct lives in the body. So when you disconnect from your instinct, the body follows. The head gets all of the energy and all of the juice. Of course it would be the only part that looks normal!" Tera paused for a sip of her tea.

"So how come you are different?" Melissa asked, leaning to spread jam on another scone.

"I don't know," Tera smiled gently. "I've never really articulated all of that before. I've always just felt like I must be different. I have felt it here," she said, pointing to her chest. "I can't explain it any better than that."

"What does it feel like?" Melissa asked, forgetting her scone. Tera sat and thought for a moment, and then she stood up.

"Come with me," Tera said, standing up. Melissa followed Tera through the apartment to a room at the back where they stood in front of two large windows. Here Tera had planted several window boxes. "It's like this," she said, digging her hands deep into the earth. She brought them out again and shook the dirt back down into the pot. Melissa followed her lead and dug her hands deeply into the dark brown earth. She didn't understand what Tera meant, but she knew that she felt a strange stirring in her chest.

"So it's about dirt?" Melissa laughed.

"No," Tera giggled. "I guess that doesn't really explain it, does it?" Tera sat down on a chair. Melissa looked around and found a bench to sit on.

"I guess it's just that I know," Tera began.

"Know what?" Melissa asked.

"That this is who I am," Tera said. When Melissa looked puzzled, Tera sighed in a gentle way and smiled a soft smile. "People always look at me strangely when I say that. But I think that when you know that, you can really get back into your body and your life. You can connect the dots."

"I wish I understood," Melissa said, watching her intently. She knew that this woman held answers to questions she didn't even know she had yet.

"Well when you know, you think differently. You know what you will and will not accept. You find kindred spirits more easily.

You can really hear your body. You can respect your cycles and be with partners who accept theirs. You begin to work on instinct rather than thought. It just gets better!" Tera grinned. "Does any of that make sense?"

"Oh, it sounds divine," Melissa nodded. "But how do you find this way of knowing?"

"I guess I just started paying attention to the wildness," Tera smiled, knowing that Melissa wouldn't understand.

"The what?" Melissa shook her head. "In any other conversation, I would think that was a ridiculous thing to say. But here, now, after all of my adventures, I feel like it must make sense."

"I think that people have forgotten where they came from," Tera smiled. Taking Melissa's hand in hers and turning it over, she showed Melissa the inside of her wrist. "Look there," Tera said. "Look at the softness of your wrist. Look at how thin the skin there is. Feel how soft and delicate you are there. Look deeper. Can you see the blood flowing through your veins? Each one of those tiny veins is pulsing with the thing that keeps you alive, just like the veins in every plant and animal. Why would we have all of that going on if we weren't wild on some level? If there wasn't some purpose to our being alive? If we didn't fit somewhere important?" Melissa stared at the place where her hand met her arm, gently rubbing her fingers over the spot, feeling the softness of the skin.

"The way I see it, every plant and animal on earth has a purpose. They all fit into things in a very specific way, so we must too. We are animals after all," Tera laughed.

"Do you know your purpose?" Melissa asked.

"Nope," Tera smiled. "But I don't think we are supposed to. Do you think that a squirrel knows what its purpose on earth is? I think that we just need to loosen our edges a little. We are so much bigger than our head realizes. I don't think we are supposed to know. But I do know that there are things I do that make me forget myself. There are things I do that make me feel like I am just living. There are things I do that make me feel like I am connected, like I am going with the flow. The trick is to feel like that as much as possible and to stop letting so much crap in."

"What things are you talking about?" Melissa asked.

"Things that just make you feel connected, brain and body, outside and inside."

"I don't understand," Melissa sighed, shaking her head.

"Are there things you do that make you lose track of time? Have you ever been doing something and then realized that you have forgotten to eat or drink or even go to the bathroom because you were so deeply involved in what you were doing?" Tera asked. Melissa shrugged her shoulders.

"Okay, let's try this another way," Tera said, taking Melissa's hand and pulling her up out of her chair. "I'll show you one of *my* things." She led Melissa out into the garden. Tera's garden was lush with growing flowers. Peonies and roses and lilies grew audaciously in every available space. Tall trees grew tightly around the edge of the garden, leaning in to offer protection to the tender blooms. Melissa could see city lights twinkling through the branches, lighting up the dew on the flowers and the grass so that everything sparkled. Melissa held her breath, not wanting to break the enchantment.

Tera led her along the rough, cold concrete of the patio and together they stepped onto the grass. It was cold and wet with dew and it tickled Melissa's bare feet.

"This is better," Melissa smiled as she let herself sink into the grass.

"What do you mean?" Tera asked.

"Well, everywhere I have been up until now on this journey has been connected to nature. Today in the city I felt lost and scared and disconnected. It's nice to feel the grass under my feet again."

"Ah, but once you feel connected to yourself it won't matter where you are," Tera smiled. Trees and grass and seas and skies are all very nice things to recharge the batteries, but you need to be able to find yourself no matter where you are. If you know who you are and you listen to your heart, anywhere can be sacred. You can filter out all of the nonsense in the world and remember what is important."

"What is important?" Melissa asked. Tera smiled a strange, faraway smile and cocked her head to one side.

"Can't you hear it?" She whispered. Her eyes twinkled as if she was listening to a beautiful song. Melissa strained and listened but she couldn't hear anything.

"Shut your eyes," Tera whispered. Melissa closed her eyes and listened. She couldn't hear anything. "Now dance," Tera said, her voice close beside Melissa's ear.

"But there isn't any music," Melissa protested.

"Yes there is. Just dance."

Melissa stood still for a long time and listened for the music. She felt silly and uncomfortable. What was she doing standing in a strange city in a strange woman's garden listening for some music that simply wasn't there? She began to move her body a little, shifting from one foot to the other, moving her arms awkwardly, but she stopped when she felt her bones begin to rattle under her skin. They knocked together, unaccustomed to the dance she was doing, feeling stiff and hard and brittle. Melissa began moving again, making her movements very small and controlled, hoping to let her body understand that she was trying to listen to it.

"Listen," she heard Tera say. Melissa opened one eye a crack and saw that Tera was dancing beside her with a look of peace on her face. Melissa wanted that look. Melissa wanted to hear whatever it was Tera was hearing, so she stopped moving. She could hear the sounds of city traffic humming all around them. There was a bird singing in one of the trees above her. An insect was buzzing around somewhere. What else could she hear?

Melissa inhaled deeply and realized that she could hear her breath. Listening as she inhaled deeply through her nose, she heard it as she opened her mouth slightly and exhaled. She could feel the softness of the air over her lips. On the next exhale she moistened her lips a little so she could feel it more intensely. She listened and felt and experienced her breath all at once. Was that what Tera had meant? Was it her own breath that she was supposed to be hearing?

Melissa listened to her breathing for a few moments before she heard something else. There was another noise coming from somewhere deep inside of her. She stopped listening to her breath and focused on the soft thumping, knowing instinctively that it was her heart. She had felt it pumping lots of times, but she couldn't remember ever actually listening to it beat before. Raising her arms up into the air beside her, her heartbeat grew louder. Feeling the urge to move, Melissa began to dance again. Moving her head from side to side she felt the tension leave her neck and shoulders.

"I think I can hear it," Melissa whispered. Tera did not answer. Melissa listened as the beat grew louder and louder in her ears. A charge ran up and down her arms and legs as blood began to reach her dry, brittle bones. Her toes and fingers and neck tingled with joy as energy, blood and heartbeat came together to add flesh. Melissa could feel as well as hear that her heart had begun to beat all over her body. Her movements were no longer small and measured, she began to twist and turn and dance in joyous ecstasy. Her heart pounded in her ears, and sweat appeared on her upper lip, forehead, under her arms and down her back. At one point her skin was the only thing holding her together as her body expanded with song and energy. Mind and pulse merged into one and for a brief moment, she knew who she was. Her heart pumped in tune with both the earth under her feet and the veins in the trees that surrounded her. Her cells blended with the energy of the city and the grass under her feet. For a moment she knew exactly where she belonged, and it was good.

A long time later Melissa took a deep breath and opened her eyes.

"There you are," Tera smiled.

Chapter Fifteen

M elissa knew she was dreaming because she was back in the forest. She was searching for something, but she had no idea what she was searching for or where it was or even why she was looking, but whatever it was, it was important and she had to find it. Counting her steps on and off the path was the only way to make sure she didn't get lost.

She had just counted six steps when a scream froze her to the spot. Crashing and shrieking, something was coming towards her through the trees. Melissa raced desperately back to her path and raced along it, trying to keep ahead of the creature following her. Every few moments she would glance behind her to see if she was getting away, but the creature was always just a few steps behind her. Hot breath was wet on the back of her neck and she could feel its fingers reaching for her. Turning to glance behind her, she could see tangled hair and wild eyes staring through even more tangles, and then Melissa was no longer afraid. She stopped running and turned towards the creature, reaching out her hands in welcome.

Melissa awoke tangled in blankets and soaked in sweat. Tera had left a light on in the bathroom and the soft glow filtered down the hallway to the living room. Melissa lay still for a few minutes absorbing what she remembered about her dream and trying to recall the moments from the previous evening. She wasn't entirely sure what had happened or even if she would ever be able to relive the feeling she had experienced, but she knew that Tera had given her a real gift. She was confident that she had learned enough now to be allowed to return home.

Padding quietly into the kitchen, Melissa poured herself a glass of water. Looking out of the window, a fierce desire to be home nearly undid her. She was tired of being in other people's kitchens. She was tired of being in the same clothes and walking this path. She was tired of lessons and meaning and not knowing what the hell was going on in her life. She was tired of living in a state of confusion. Her little apartment and her little ordinary life looked very appealing from here. Surely this was all some sort of weird *Wizard of Oz* trip and all she had to do was open her eyes and everyone she loved would be there and no time would have passed. Wishing she could just click her heels, she became desperate to get home.

Tera had left some towels on one of the chairs for her. Melissa gratefully took them to the bathroom and got cleaned up, vowing to never take another shower or bath for granted again. Tiptoeing into the kitchen she fixed herself a small breakfast of tea and toast. After last night she didn't feel like very much. She was too busy trying to pull together the feelings she was having of being lighter and heavier all at the same time.

"Make sure you take a few scones for the trip," Tera said as she stepped into the kitchen and sat down on a bench. She was wrapped in a fluffy white robe.

"Good morning," Melissa said.

"Not quite," Tera grinned sleepily.

"I'm sorry to wake you," Melissa smiled back.

"No, no, I don't mind. I'll just go back to bed in a minute!"

"Thank you for everything," Melissa whispered, feeling quite shy now that they were saying goodbye.

"You're welcome," Tera said, getting up and giving Melissa a quick hug. "Have a safe rest of your journey!"

Melissa packed a few scones wrapped in napkins into the top of her bag. Putting her worn shoes back on, she shouldered her bag and paused at the front door.

"Thanks again," she smiled at Tera. "I won't forget you!"

"Well I should hope not," Tera laughed. "How many perfect strangers' doors do you knock on in your life?"

"Not many," Melissa laughed back. "Not many at all." With a small wave, she opened the front door and stepped through. As she crossed the threshold, the world spun wildly around her and her stomach flipped over. Closing her eyes, she waited.

The door was gone. The city was gone too. Instead of a city stoop, Melissa was now standing on the top of a hill. A path stretched down away from her in both directions. She had assumed that after being with Tera, she would have learned everything she needed to learn. She had assumed that she would now be safely walking towards home. From what she could see, nothing was further from the truth.

Chapter Sixteen

S he saw it before she saw him.

Her path had begun to dry out. Rocky and difficult were words that could have been used to describe both the way and her mood. Matters did not improve when she walked straight up to a pile of lumber. Circling the pile, she could not see her path on the other side. Patience in tatters, she raised her eyes to the sky.

"Are you kidding me?" She shouted. Flinging her bag to the ground, she sat on the pile of wood and held her head in her hands knowing that there was nothing she could do. Nothing that had happened so far was an accident. Before she could go any further, she was going to have to do something in order to learn another lesson, and sitting here was just going to prolong the issue. Grinding her teeth together in frustration, she decided to get started.

Smooth and dusty, the lumber was the colour of cold butter. It was so fresh and new that it felt wrong that someone had left in on the ground. A brand new hammer and bright red toolbox glinted at her from the top of the pile. Shaking her head in disgust, Melissa turned to look for other clues. Behind her there was now a squat lean-to that she knew for a fact hadn't been there before. Walking under its eaves, a smell stopped her cold. For an instant she was back in her grandfather's workshop watching him make her a birdhouse. If she closed her eyes, she could feel him hugging her, the cotton of his shirt soft under her cheek; her nose filled with his scent: sawdust and tools and fresh air. It was all too much and she stumbled back outside.

"What is it you want me to do?" She hollered to the sky.

"Build a house," came the answer. Never having had an actual answer to one of her questions before, Melissa turned around wildly. That was when she finally saw him.

"Hi," he said, walking towards her with his hand outstretched. Instead of shaking it, Melissa just looked at him. "I'm Eli," he said, reaching out his hand again.

"Melissa," she answered, weakly shaking his hand. It had been a very long time since she had last spoken to a man, and Eli was most definitely a man. Slightly shaggy brown hair curled around his head, making the perfect frame for his face. His brown eyes sparkled as he looked at her, noticing her looking him over. Dressed simply in jeans and a black t-shirt, he certainly looked strong enough to build a house. When she looked at his face again, she saw that his lips were moving.

"I'm sorry. Pardon?" Melissa said, clearing her vision so that she could focus on him.

"I asked if you were okay. You seem a little out of it."

"No, fine, thank you." Melissa said, giving herself a shake. "Sorry, you said I was supposed to build a house?"

"Well, that's what the note says," he began.

"Note?" Melissa was paying attention now. She'd never had a note before.

"Yes, it was addressed to you. It's there, on the tool box." Eli led her over to where the toolbox sat. Gleaming and red, the toolbox looked out of place in the beige world of lumber and earth. Sure enough, there was an envelope on top. Snatching it from the box, Melissa held it with trembling fingers.

"See, it's addressed to you," Eli pointed. Melissa did indeed see her name written in large, wobbly letters across the front of the yellowed envelope. Suddenly she couldn't breathe. She recognized this note. She recognized it because she had written it to herself.

"What is it?" Eli asked, moving to comfort her. Melissa's sharp look stopped him.

"You read this?" Melissa asked him bitterly.

"I did," he answered without an explanation. Melissa ran her fingers across the letters. She knew them by heart.

"To: Melissa Elizabeth Owens. From: Myself at eleven to Myself at twenty-one."

"Aren't you going to open it?" Eli asked. Defensiveness filled her mouth like lemon juice.

"Why? You already have."

"No, I didn't." Eli said, sticking his hands deeply into his jeans pockets.

"But you said..." she started. Before she could finish, he turned and walked towards the pile of lumber.

Sure enough, the flap on the envelope was still glued shut. Melissa remembered the day that she had written this letter. She had been reading *Emily Climbs* by L.M. Montgomery and wanted to copy Emily in writing a letter to herself when she was older. In the years since she had forgotten about the letter and it had been lost. At twenty-one she hadn't even remembered to look for it.

The glue gave way easily and she was soon lost in the world and the questions of her eleven year-old self.

Was she married to Nathan? Had she and Alice really gone to Australia after high school? Was she a famous actress or a veterinarian? Had her boobs ever grown in? Had her parents stopped driving her crazy? It must be lovely to be old enough to never eat broccoli. Did she still love to read and what were her favourite books now? Who had she become now that she was a grown up?

Ghosts and memories teased and tore at Melissa's heart as she read. Turning the page, she found what she thought Eli must have read.

Dear Twenty-one, I know that you probly think I am a little girl and are to grown up to listen to me, but I want to make sure you remember how much you need YOUR OWN SPACE. I hop that you have a house of your own. This is what I want to build in the back yard if Daddy will let me. Underneath were a number of drawings and scribbles designing her perfect house. She had written that it only needed two rooms: one for resting and one for playing. Big scratchy arrows pointed at each one, making it clear which was which. Underneath at the bottom was scrawled: *I hop you have a house like this somday. I hop you are happy. I love you. I hop you remember me. Love Eleven.*

Her parents had said no.

Build a house. It was a clear instruction. What neither the note nor the instruction had mentioned was Eli, and Melissa didn't know what to do with him. As far back as she could remember she had had to figure things out on her own. When she had taken other people's opinions into account so far, it had only delayed her. It was only when she had started listening to her own intuition and believing in her own instincts that she had begun to make progress. As lonely as it had been at times, she knew that she was on the right track. Now there was Eli. Strong, capable and willing to help, he seemed to know what she needed to do. Wanting desperately to get this right and keep moving, his attempts to help only infuriated her.

"You should hold the nail like this or you are going to hit your fingers."

"Thank you Eli, I have used a hammer before."

"I think that we should look at how much lumber there is. We don't want to run out half-way through."

"It's not going to be very big, I am sure that there will be enough. I just want to get started."

"Here, let me carry that for you."

"Thank you Eli, but I am perfectly capable of carrying it myself." Every time she moved, he was there with her, trying to help. Every time she made a decision, he would question her, knowing somehow better than she did what she needed to do. It would be easier, she knew, to let him take over or to let him do it. Always having prided herself on being a strong, capable woman, it was driving her crazy even thinking of handing things over.

"Eli, thank you, but I can do this myself," she smiled through gritted teeth as he tried for the hundredth time to help her.

"Fine!" He said, throwing up his hands with frustration equal to hers and storming away towards the woods. Melissa watched him go with guilt stinging her mouth. Not wanting to make this last any longer than it needed to, she went back to work, leaving a deep scar in the ground as she dragged a board over to where she had begun building her house.

Her splinters had splinters and apparently thumbs did not approve of being thwacked repeatedly with a hammer. For three days and most of three nights Melissa had been building what she now wasn't able to honestly call a house. Having no idea how to build anything, she had called on her memories of *Extreme Makeover Home Edition* re-runs. In her mind she was building a cute little cottage to fit in the corner of her childhood garden and it would all be done in seven days. In the meantime, however, muscles she didn't know she had hurt, she hadn't seen Eli in three days and what she was building looked more like the skeleton of a misshapen outhouse than a cute cottage. It was not going well.

"Okay, how good does this have to be?" She asked no one in particular, hammering a nail into what she hoped looked a little bit like a window frame. "I know that I can't move on until I have completed this challenge, but I really suck at this." As if to prove her point, the piece of wood that had been making up the top of the window escaped from its nails and bounced off of her head. Dazed, Melissa half fell, half sat down on the marred ground beneath her. Hot tears blinded her as she held her hand to the top of her head. Slightly hysterical and wanting somehow to retaliate for the pain she was in, she gave the wall of the house a fierce kick. She wasn't sure if she was because she was concussed, but all at once the world around her seemed to be in slow motion. Cracking and groaning as its joints gave way, her house began to lean in the direction of her kick. Although the motion was slow, it wasn't long before the whole thing lay in crumpled agony on the ground. With a strangled noise, Melissa joined it, unable to do anything but lie on the ground and cry.

"I give up," she whispered.

Crackling roused her. It wasn't the same crackling that the house had made; this was cheerier and more welcoming. Hours spent in a depressed heap had made her cold and sore and night had drawn in when she wasn't paying attention. Sitting up and stretching, she traced the crackling to a small campfire and to Eli.

"Hello," she said sheepishly, sitting beside him.

"How are you?" He asked, standing with his arms crossed. Melissa wondered whether he was protecting himself from her.

"Sorry," she whispered. "I should have let you help. I really didn't know what I was doing."

"What do you mean?" He smiled, leaning back to view the crumpled heap now barely visible in the gloom.

"I really thought I needed to do it by myself," Melissa shrugged.

"Who in their right mind would expect anyone to be able to build a house by themselves?" He asked, arching a gorgeous eyebrow at her. She stared at it, taking in what he had said. When she finally looked at his eyes, she saw that he was laughing.

"Don't laugh at me," she snapped.

"I'm not," he protested. "But tell me why you would choose to do something like that by yourself." Melissa thought about his question for a long time. Staring into the flames she thought back to all of the times that she had struggled through because she had wanted to prove that she was capable of doing something herself – especially with the men in her life.

"Why is it weak to accept help?" He asked, looking directly at her.

"It's not about being weak, it's about being strong and capable," she said, as much to herself as to him.

"As who?" He asked.

"As you."

"Who says you aren't?" He snorted. "Who do you think is stronger? The person who tries to do everything even when they don't know how, or the person who asks for help and then learns as they go?"

"Whatever," she spat, not looking at him and feeling tight rage holding her chest. Defences well and truly up, Melissa prepared to shut the conversation down.

"Melissa, what do you really want?" He asked. Not waiting for an answer, he set off in search of more scraps of wood to put on the fire, leaving Melissa's blustering defences behind.

Working up a sharp answer, Melissa fumed and grumbled to herself for a few moments. Who did he think he was? Righteous anger bubbled, but a very small voice began to filter through the darkness. What did she want? When the question finally dug through, she was left without any anger at all. What *did* she want?

Even the rain couldn't dampen their enthusiasm. After a fitful night beside the fire, Melissa and Eli woke to a tentative truce. Without talking about the night before, they got up and began building. At first, every time Eli tried to help, Melissa would have to bite her tongue to stop herself from snapping at him, but as the day went on she had to admit that he made things a lot easier. By lunchtime they were laughing together, and by the time they stopped for something to eat at the end of the day, the sparkle and colour had returned to Eli's face.

"Now, was that so bad?" Eli asked as he pulled a sweater over his head.

"No," Melissa admitted with a smile. It wasn't until much later that she let herself think about his question again, and again it kept her awake long into the night.

It had taken them three days, but the house was just about done. Standing back to admire their handiwork, Melissa couldn't help but think that there was something missing.

"It doesn't look quite finished," Eli said. "Hang on a minute." Smiling with intent, he walked over to the lean-to and came back with a board in his hands. "For you," he grinned, handing it over. Melissa laughed when she saw that he had made a sign for her door. In large purple letters, the sign read: *Melissa Owens, age 11*. Looking back at Eli, Melissa held the sign up to the door and asked him the question he had been waiting for since he had met her.

"Can you help me?"

"Love to," he grinned. Together, they hammered the sign in its rightful place above the door. Melissa stepped back to view her house.

"Dear eleven-year-old self," she whispered. "Now we both have a place of our own. I hope you like it." Energy shot through her body, making her shiver with joy and power. Now the only left to do was go inside.

"I know what it is I want," Melissa smiled.

"I'm glad," Eli grinned.

"I always want to feel like this."

"What does it feel like?"

"Empowered," she said. "Thank you for helping me get here."

"Any time!" Eli smiled with one corner of his mouth and his eyes sparkled. "Are you going in?"

"Come with me?" Melissa asked, grabbing his hand. Energy shot through her body again and noise like a gunshot echoed through the clearing. Wobbling on her feet for a moment, Melissa threw her arms open to steady herself as a wave of heat and power engulfed her. Wondering where Eli was, she bent over for a moment to allow her vision and senses to clear. When she finally stood upright again, he was gone.

"Eli?" At the same moment she called for him, she knew he was already there. He was not beside her or near her, but within her. The strong feelings she had felt in the garden with Tera were back again, but now there was a different energy standing firmly alongside them. Melissa fell to the ground weeping with the enormity of her feelings. For the first time in as long as she could remember, she felt balanced.

She felt whole.

It was a very different Melissa who got to her feet a few breaths later. Pausing only to pick up her bag and to give a smile and a wink to the purple sign, she bent and stepped through the door to her house. It was without surprise that on the other side of the door she found only the path up the mountain.

Chapter Seventeen

The path sloped steadily upward. The ground under her feet was dry and rough and covered with loose gravel and larger stones and rocks. Melissa stopped for a moment to catch her breath and look around, rubbing her neck with one dusty hand. For days now she had been concentrating on the path ahead, keeping her eyes firmly focused on the ground to keep from slipping and falling on the loose stones. Finally giving in to how tired and sore she was, she took a minute to stretch and look around her. Shivering in the cold, thin air, she checked her skin for goosebumps, but all she could see was the layer of filth that covered her. How long had it been since she had had a wash? How long had it been since she had realized that she needed one?

Lifting her hands to her face she wearily rubbed her eyes. Knowing that her face must be just as dirty as the rest of her, she tried to picture her own face. Scrunching up her forehead in concentration she realized that she had no idea what she looked like anymore. A framed picture of her had once sat on her mother's piano. Did she look like that? The picture was a few years old now, and felt like it had been taken of someone else. How could she not remember?

Using her fingers, she traced the contours of her face, following the hollows of her eye sockets and the soft, whispering kiss of her eyelashes. She traced the lines of her eyebrows and down the length of her nose. Flattening her fingers together, she felt the broad expanse of her forehead and then separated her hands to caress down to her cheeks. Turning her hands over, she traced circles over her cheekbones for a few moments, moving up towards her ear and back down to her nose. Still using the backs of her hands, she felt along the length of her chin, down to her throat and back up again. Finally, with the tips of four fingers she traced her lips. She felt the dip where they reached out for her nose, and the fullness of her bottom lip. Opening her mouth, she let her breath touch her fingertips for a moment. Gently, she breathed in and out, enjoying the warmth on her cold skin. The tip of her tongue slipped through her lips, tracing the top of her middle finger and tasting the dusty saltiness of her skin. Taking a deep breath, she exhaled sharply and ran both hands over her face as if washing it. There was nothing else to do but keep going.

For the first time in days, the view ahead of her was different. A large rock face completely blocked her way. As she walked closer, she could see that her path actually led into a crack in the rock. Blinded by sunshine, she could not see how high up the top was, but she could see that a crevasse crept away in front of her. The walls were high and the path was rocky, but it was clearly the next part of her journey. She adjusted the straps on her bag, and stepped through the opening.

The air was wet and icy. Ferns and grasses grew in nooks and crannies closer to the top of the crevasse, and the walls were green and slimy with seepage and moss. The ground below her was slippery and she had to step carefully to avoid falling. She tried to hold her hands against the walls to steady herself, but they were soon covered in green and brown slime. Lacking the will to care about being clean, she wiped her hands on her legs and kept moving forward.

In some places the crevasse widened and she was able to step back and try to get a good look at the top. In other places the way was so tight, she had to take off her bag and go through sideways. Soon her whole body was covered in slime and mud.

"There has got to be an easier way," she exclaimed out loud as she squeezed her body through a particularly narrow opening. Grunting as she pushed herself through, she finally let out her breath. The noise she made startled a bird that had been on the floor of the crevasse ahead of her and it took off in a flurry of feathers, straight up and out into the sky. Melissa stood still in shock, her mouth hanging open and her bag still hanging in her outstretched hand. She had not seen a living creature since the bumblebee in the garden. Before that she had not seen one at all. Flattening herself against the wall, she bent her head back as far as it would go, desperate to catch another glimpse of the bird. For the first time she could see the top of the crevasse. As she looked, the bird flew overhead, flying from one side of the opening to the other. Melissa's cry of excitement caught in her throat and tears filled her eyes. She rested her head against the wall and took several deep breaths, the air wet in her lungs. Knowing she was on the right track, she started walking again.

Melissa felt the first drop of rain on the tip of her nose. It stopped her short and as she wiped it off she looked up to see where the drop had come from. Another drop fell on her arm. She looked as high as she could. The sky above her was a light, bright blue. No rain clouds hovered, and yet she was getting wet. A few more drops fell onto her skin. She was surprised to feel that the rain felt warm on her cold skin. Turning her face upwards again she felt more droplets land and then slide across her face. One landed on her lip. Instinctively she traced the spot with her tongue, but stopped when she realized that the drop was salty. She held out her hand to catch one of the drops. Lifting her palm to her mouth, she tasted the caught rain with the tip of her tongue. Sure enough, the rain tasted of tears.

It was only a few moments later that she reached the end of the path. She had been concentrating on her feet when she realized that a wall blocked her way. She had come to the end of the crevasse, but instead of coming out on the other side, she had reached another rock face. She touched the wall directly in front of her, hoping that it wasn't real. Now what? She pushed and pulled on it, hoping for a hidden door. There had to be a reason for her to have come this far. She couldn't believe that this whole journey had been towards a dead end.

Nothing moved.

Melissa turned around and around in circles trying to see a way out. She walked a little way back up the path, looking more closely at the walls, and hoping that she had just missed another passage. When she found nothing, she returned to the end and looked up again. Dropping her bag on the slimy ground, she looked up in time to see another bird fly across the visible piece of sky. Frustrated, she leaned against the wall, sliding down until she sat on the wet floor, ignoring the cold water seeping through her clothes. The rain continued to fall gently, making the slime even worse.

She waited, hoping that at some point she would get some sort of sign. Maybe someone else would come up the path towards her. Maybe something would fall from the sky. There had to be some way around or through all of this. Should she go back to the beginning of the crevasse? Maybe she should have looked around some more at the entrance. Maybe there was another way that she should have taken. Shivering as the reality and the dampness finally took hold of her, she rummaged in the bag beside her for another layer and discovered a neatly folded sweatshirt. Looking around, she stood and got changed in the small space, smiling at the absurdity of making sure no one was looking.

As she pulled the shirt over her head, she glanced at the wall in front of her. Pulling the fabric down around her, she stepped forward and looked more closely at the wall. There was something sticking out of the rock about two feet from the ground. It was just a piece of rock but it had been painted dark green and had been jammed into a small crack in the face. She pulled on it but it wouldn't budge. Looking more closely she saw that there was another piece pushed into the rock about a foot higher than that, which was also painted dark green. In fact, when she looked at the wall from a slight angle she could see that there were many of these rocks sticking out of the surface, each about a foot higher than the last. You couldn't see them unless you were looking for them, but they were there. Melissa reached for the one just above the level of her head and tested it with her full weight. It held.

"I'm supposed to climb this," she murmured. Looking slowly up as far as she could see, she was suddenly very aware of where she was. Claustrophobia grasped at her ankles, and she became desperate to be out in the air and the sunshine. Pulling her bag onto her shoulders she carefully put one foot on the first step. Reaching up, she gripped the closest one with her fingers and pulled her body against the wall. Holding her breath, she reached up for the next step and tried to pull herself towards it. Her fingers slipped and she lost her footing, knocking her knee against the wall, she fell back onto the ground. Pain shot through her from all directions, and it took her a moment to catch her breath.

"I must do this," she whispered to herself. Gingerly, she put her foot on the first step again and reached for the step closest to her head, pulling herself onto the wall. This time she slid her other foot onto the next step before she moved her hands. Legs stronger than her fingers, she soon realized that she needed to use their strength to keep her on the wall. Balancing herself with her hands, she climbed, only making it a few feet before her toes slipped off again. She almost caught herself, but the motion shifted the load on her back, and the weight pulled her to the ground again.

Melissa lay still for a moment, letting the pain have its way. A close inspection found that one of her elbows was cut and bleeding, but other than that, she knew that she had only been bruised. Pulling the straps on her bag more securely to her body, she stepped back towards the wall. Again she stepped on the stone, and again she reached up for a handhold. Pulling herself against the wall, she moved her foot so that she was standing on the inside of her foot instead of on her toes. Moving her other leg, she did the same thing on the next step. Slowly and painfully she pulled and pushed herself upwards, scraping her stomach against the rocks, making an agonizingly slow climb towards the surface.

Pausing for a moment, Melissa tried to catch her breath. Her body shuddered as she gasped for air. Her legs and arms were screaming in pain and her shoulders ached from the effort of carrying her heavy bag. Resting her head against the wall for a moment, the cold slime of the rock felt strangely comforting against her forehead. The weight of her bag was pulling her back towards the ground but she moved one of her hands to ease her cramped fingers, nearly losing her balance. Pulling herself closer to the wall, she held on, tasting blood where she had ground her teeth against her cheek. With only her will left with enough energy to move; she forced her exhausted body to keep going. Inch by painful inch, she moved closer to the top.

As she reached for one of the steps, she yelped in surprise. Her fingers had found something round and hard. Jamming her feet as tightly to the rock as she could, she took the thing in her fingers and brought it down so that she could see it. Closer inspection showed that she had found a beeswax candle. There was a vague memory in her head of seeing them made at a museum when she was a little girl, and she lifted it to her nose, inhaling the familiar scent of sunshine and honey. All she had been able to smell for days was dampness and stone, so this smell was nearly her undoing. Fighting back tears, she fumbled around with one hand and managed to stick the candle into one of the side pockets of her backpack. Shifting the bag this way nearly pulled her off balance, but she recovered and started moving again.

A raindrop fell on her cheek and she looked up, not feeling like she was getting anywhere. She stopped and opened and closed the fingers on her right hand. They had started to fizz with pain. Biting back tears she reached up again and let out another cry. There was something on this step as well! This time it felt hard and square, and she was startled to see that it was a small book. Bracing herself against the wall she held it out so that she could see what it was, rolling her eyes a little when she discovered that it was a beginners guide to mountain climbing. Slowly and carefully she manoeuvred so that she could get it into her bag as well. With one hand she tried to pull on the zipper, but this small motion made her exhausted feet scramble to stay on the rocks. Hugging the wall as tightly as she could, she was able to keep herself from falling, but she bashed her other elbow in the process. Breathing deeply, she remained still for a few minutes before beginning again.

The rain started to fall more steadily and the way became more and more slippery. Just as Melissa was certain that she could not go on any longer, her hand found a ledge instead of a step. Looking up, she could see that the ledge was fairly wide and she hoped that it was deep enough to hold her. Asking her legs for just a little more energy, she climbed until she could pull herself into a sitting position, finding the ledge to be big enough to hold her. Shrugging her bag from her shoulders, she put it beside her, enjoying the relief that came from taking the load from her back. She wriggled herself back so that she could rest against the rock face but found her way blocked by something soft. Too tired to be afraid, she reached behind her and pulled out a blanket. Melissa stared at it for a few minutes, not comprehending what it was or why it was there. Then without thinking or wondering or asking, she leaned up against the cliff wall, wrapped the blanket around her, and went to sleep.

It was the rain that woke her. She had no idea how long she had been sleeping or what time of day it was. Every muscle in her body ached and the bottoms of her feet felt bruised. Painfully, she straightened her legs and unwrapped herself from the blanket. The top didn't look very far away now. If she could just force her body to do a little bit more, she might just make it up there. Opening her bag, she folded the damp blanket and stuffed it inside. When she pulled the bag onto her back, her shoulders protested sharply.

"We don't have far to go," she whispered to her body. "Please, let's just do this and then we can rest at the top." Perched on the edge of the ledge, she peered towards the ground. It looked gloomy and damp down there, so she looked up at the sky. Every fibre and every cell in her body yearned to be up on top. She didn't know what was up there but she knew that it had to be better than it was down here. Standing, she reached for the next step, finding something there waiting for her. Reaching up, she pulled down a bottle filled with water.

"Oh, thank you!" She whispered to anyone who could hear her. She opened the top of the bottle and then brought the edge to her lips. Cold, clear water poured over her tongue and down her throat. Swallowing greedily, she could feel the water feeding the cells in her body. With a sigh she smiled and put the top back on the bottle, stuffing it inside one of the bag's side pockets and reaching up for the next step.

No matter what she did she could not seem to get a grip. Her bag grew heavier and heavier on her shoulders and every muscle in her body ached with every movement. The top was closer now, but the weight she carried had become too much for her to bear. She stopped several times to adjust the straps, but she could not get them to sit properly and she wondered if she could stop somehow and adjust the load. She thought about climbing back down to the ledge and repacking the blanket, but she just wanted the climb to be over.

Letting go of the rock with her left hand, she tugged at the strap over her right shoulder. The load shifted violently to the right and her body was pulled to the side. Melissa cursed as she lost her balance and swung out over the hole. Only her right foot and hand kept her from falling. The bag slipped down and dangled from her elbows, nearly pulling her from her precarious perch. Cursing, Melissa grabbed the rock more tightly with her right hand. The bag was tugging her downwards so she pulled her left arm free in an attempt to gain enough motion to get a better grip. With both hands she clung to the same piece of rock, but her right arm was now taking the full weight of her bag. Letting go of the rock with her right hand, she tried to slide the bag down to her hand so that she could get a grip on the straps and for a moment she had it in her hand. Balancing carefully, she tried to manoeuvre the bag back towards her shoulder but the movement made one of her feet slip. In that instant, she grabbed for the wall with her right hand and lost her grip on the bag. It slipped silently away into the gloom below.

Melissa clung to the wall for a moment, helplessly waiting for it all not to have happened. Tears blinded her and the walls echoed with her cry of agony and frustration. Above her she could see the top of the crevasse and the patch of blue sky. Below her she could feel the damp darkness. With a mournful sound, she started to climb back down the wall.

Down was easier than up. Her body knew the way down already and Melissa did not have to concentrate as hard. Despair and frustration nearly swallowed her and she forced herself to climb back into the darkness without looking up again. Passing the ledge only a few minutes after beginning her descent, she allowed herself a glimmer of hope when she saw something sitting on it. For a moment she hoped her bag had been caught there, but she was devastated to see that it was not there. Pausing for a rest, she realized that the thing that she had thought was her bag was a blanket. She clearly remembered packing the one from this morning in her bag. How did it get back to the ledge? Numbly, she shook her head and continued to climb downwards.

A few hours later her foot found solid ground. Melissa pushed herself away from the wall and collapsed on the ground in a heap, tears joining with the salty rain. She couldn't believe that she was back here at the bottom. The rain washed clear lines across her filthy cheeks and hands and soaked into her clothes and hair, but she didn't move.

It was the damp ground that finally forced her up. Her muscles, so tired from their climb, finally protested over the hard, cold surface they were lying on. Melissa could see her bag lying on the ground a few feet from where she was sitting so she crawled towards it and pulled it onto her lap. It was empty.

Frantically, she searched the ground for the things that had been in her bag. She remembered the blanket, the candle, the bottle of water, the book, and the other things that she had put into the bag starting from the beginning of her journey. She remembered her red shoes and Lola's matches and Elle's scarf and Grace's compass and Delia's honey. None of these things were in her bag any longer. She hadn't needed them since she'd put them in so she hadn't really paid any attention to whether or not they were in there. Resting her head against the rock, she let the tears come again, shaking her head in disbelief. She had come all of this way back for an empty bag.

"What is this all about?" She screeched as loud as she could. Her desperation and fury needed a voice. Wanting to fling the bag against the rocks, Melissa pulled on it, but this time it felt heavy. Opening it, she found it full of rocks.

"Very funny," she yelled, standing up and shaking her fist in the air. "Do you hear me? I said very funny!"

"So what am I supposed to do now?" She barked at the walls, trembling with frustration and anger. Not knowing who to direct her anger at, she decided to take it out on herself. She had chosen to climb back down into the hole after a bag. Hadn't Selene told her that all she had was all she needed? Why had she accepted so much along the way that had weighed her down? Every time she had opened the bag she had found what she needed, why had she felt the need to collect more things? Melissa decided that all of this was her own stupid fault for making the bag so heavy in the first place.

Angry tears still flowed down her cheeks when she turned to face the wall. Out of habit she picked up her bag and looked into it once more, but once again there was nothing inside. She held it for a moment and then let it drop to the ground. Without another glance downward, Melissa began to climb the wall again.

Using the first attempt as a guide, she used what it had taught her. She stepped onto each rock with the inside of her foot and used her legs to take her weight and to propel her upwards, using her hands to keep herself as close to the wall as possible. Without the bag to weigh her down it was much easier for her to find balance and to keep herself centred. Ignoring the pain from her feet and hands, she climbed higher and higher up the wall. Several times she lost her grip and nearly slipped, but she kept her hold. When she thought she was too tired to go on, she rested her cheek against the wall and took several deep breaths. From somewhere she found a little bit more energy.

She knew she was getting close to the ledge when her fingers brushed against something hard and round. Sure enough, there was a beeswax candle waiting on one of the steps. She looked at it for a moment, but realized that she didn't need to carry it up any higher. When she found the book on climbing she laughed out loud. Why would she have picked that up the first time when she was already climbing? When she got to the ledge she stopped and gave herself a rest. Wrapping the blanket around her weary body, she curled in the tiny space and let herself fall into a much-needed sleep.

As soon as she was awake, she reached up to the next step where she remembered finding the bottle of water. Sure enough, it was waiting for her. After drinking her fill, she left the bottle on the ledge. Squaring her shoulders and gritting her teeth, she climbed back out onto the wall. This was the part of the climb that had been the hardest for her the first time. Her muscles strained and pulled, and she could feel every joint pushing its limits. Her brow furrowed with determination as sweat poured down her face and back. She paused for a moment and looked up. The top was close enough now that she could see grass growing at the edge. She glanced down at where she had come. It was a bit clearer today and she could see the crumpled red heap that was her knapsack. She wondered if there was anything in it now.

"We can do this," she muttered to her body. "Just a few more steps and we'll be there." Her body responded by finding just a little bit more energy from somewhere deep inside. Slowly, painfully and carefully she move steadily upwards until her right hand felt grass. She was nearly there. Her pounding heart pushed her through the last few feet, and as soon as she could, she bent double at the waist and rolled herself forward onto the grass, not stopping until she was well away from the edge.

"I did it," she whispered to the sky. Fatigue and pain kept her from moving any farther. The sun shone warmly on her face, and she smiled as a bird flew overhead. "I did it."

Chapter Eighteen

Long and soft, the grass held her gently. Part of her wanted to lie there forever, but just as she had begun to relax, the grass began tickling at her cheeks and arms. Not for the first time, Melissa became acutely aware of time ticking by. Was the grass actually growing around her? With a groan, she pulled herself onto all fours. Her path didn't end here. Ahead of her was an open field and then a great whispering wall of forest, and she knew her path led her back amongst the trees.

She wanted to rest. She wanted to stop there and lick her wounds. She wanted to allow the bruises and the cuts to heal. But the path continued on. Every step she took brought her closer to home. The dark, damp place she had just crawled out of was behind her and she was not willing to sit at the edge of it any longer. Clawing at the grass in front of her, she pulled herself up. Her feet thudded in protest, but she dug down as deeply as she could.

"Please keep going," she whispered silently to her beleaguered body and it responded with a small flicker of energy. Sagging with exhaustion and placing one foot in front of the other, she found her way back to her path. Although she was at the edge of her endurance, she realized that this place felt right. Her feet knew that she needed to be here. Her legs responded by moving her forward. She was on the right track and she needed to keep going.

A bird flew overhead and Melissa exclaimed with delight. She watched it fly towards the cover of the trees and her pace quickened when she realized that she could hear other birds singing in the treetops. Cocking her head to one side, she listened. There was magic in those trees. With a determined smile on her face she started to walk again. There were brambles and bushes between the field and the forest, but she kept going. Thorns tried to stop her and branches tugged her back, but she pushed through. Nothing was going to slow her down this time. She was almost there.

The forest air was soft and cool on her skin, and she felt easier under the cover of its branches. Trees burst greenly around her, shooting up into the air with the exuberance of the young. The crisp white and black of the birches stood out against the soft silvers and browns of the poplars and maples. Together they grew, long and lean, nestling together in their leaves high overhead. The grasses and ferns grew high between the trees, and they reached forward and tickled her legs gently as she passed. It was light and playful here. She felt them giving her breath. When she smiled a greeting to the trees they rustled back at her, encouraging her to keep moving.

"There's more," the leaves whispered in her ear.

"Go deeper," the trunks groaned in the wind.

Melissa did not linger at the edge of the woods, no matter how light it had made her heart. The trees were right. There was something deeper in the woods, something there that was just for her.

"I'm going!" She boldly called to the treetops.

Melissa lost all track of time. The light changed as she walked closer to the heart of the forest. The trees began to grow closer together, branches tangling with one another overhead. There was no gleeful rustling here. The further along the path she walked, the more still the forest became. The ground around her no longer supported light grasses and now a thick layer of orange needles and discarded branches and leaves muffled the passage of her feet. Branches snapped when she stepped on them, the noise startling her and making her pay more attention. Here and there a tree lay on its side, having come to the end of its life. It was only in these places that direct sunlight shone. In the sudden burst of light, ferns and mushrooms took advantage of the fallen tree so that even in death, the tree gave life.

These older trees also spoke to Melissa. She felt their messages like the beat of a drum in her chest. Keep going. Keep moving. This is right. This is yours. You are almost home.

"Thank you," she said quietly. That small sound felt strange and she realized that she did not need to thank them. Her own heart thudded her gratitude. They knew. They could feel it too.

The deeper Melissa walked, the quieter the forest became, and she fought the urge to hold her breath. She wanted to be as silent as the trees, but she knew that her breath was a gift from them and she needed to take as much of it in as possible. She was more tired than she had ever been in her life, but her instincts had taken over so she kept moving, kept breathing, kept following, and her body responded with energy to keep going deeper and deeper into the forest.

Melissa felt as much as heard the silence and knew that she had come to the centre. The trees around her grew wide and strong, their ancient limbs gnarled with years. She stopped walking and closed her eyes. The only thing she felt or heard was the soft in and out of her breath. The trees no longer spoke, but all around her was a language that she felt she had known once. Silence deepened and widened until it was holding her and letting her go at the same time. Her breath swirled deeper and deeper into her body as she took it all in.

Melissa opened her eyes and looked around her. Wanting to go deeper, she took one more step. An enormous gnarled oak tree filled the path in front of her. Tangled up in its roots was a small house, its thick walls bulging under the weight of the ancient tree. The roof that peeked out amongst the roots was covered in moss and pieces of bark. Melissa could see that there was a window on each side of the front door, but she couldn't see through them. The windows were made up of dozens of pieces of oddly shaped glass shining in iridescent purples and blues and greens. Or was it yellows and oranges and reds? A chimney stuck out between two of the tree's roots and a plume of lavender smoke curled out of the top. Melissa's path led right up to the front door.

As if it were the most natural thing in the world, Melissa knocked on the front door. A woman nearly as ancient as the tree appeared, her whole face lit up with a welcoming smile.

"I've been waiting for you," she said.

Chapter Nineteen

Walking through the house, Melissa stole glances through doorways into different rooms, surprised by the number of faces she saw. Passing one door she paused for a moment, thinking that she recognized the woman in the room. The woman looked up and smiled at her, sending Melissa scuttling away in embarrassment.

The house was much larger than it had looked from the outside.

The deeper they went into the house, the more Melissa had the feeling that she had been there before. She knew the faces of the women that stood in the doorways. She knew what colour the rooms would be painted before she walked by them, and that the kitchen would be at the back of the house. She knew that the floor would be warm to the touch and that sometimes the walls shook with music. She knew where her room would be. She knew. Deep in her bones she knew, and it frightened her.

The woman led her to the only door in the house that was closed. Behind it they found a large bathtub. Melissa nearly sobbed in gratitude and relief.

"There is a place there where you can wash your clothes," the woman said. "If you do that first, I will hang them by the fire to dry while you are in the bathtub. I have a feeling you will be in there for a little while," she smiled and went out, shutting the door behind her, revealing a fluffy white robe hanging from a hook.

Melissa began to strip off her filthy clothes. One by one pieces of clothing fell into a heap on the floor. Profound weariness took her over as she pulled the fluffy robe over her bare skin. All she wanted to do was clean her body but she knew that she needed something to put on afterwards and she couldn't bear to think of putting her dirty things on again. Along the side of the room was a counter that held four sinks, each already full of water. There was also an assortment of soaps and detergents in pots and bottles. Piece by piece she put her clothes into the sinks to soak and beginning with her long sleeved shirt, she began to scrub the filth from the fabric. She washed and scrubbed and rinsed and squeezed her clothes until the water coming out of them ran clear.

Melissa put her wet clothes into a pile on the counter and moved to sit on the edge of the bathtub. There was a knock at the door.

"Are they ready?" The woman asked, opening the door and moving into the room.

"Yes, thank you," Melissa smiled, moving to pick them up and hand them to her. "I'm sorry, I've not introduced myself. I'm Melissa."

"I know," the woman smiled. Melissa expected her to introduce herself but the woman just took the pile of clothes and quietly left the room, pulling the door shut behind her.

Melissa was too excited about her bath to think about anything else. She ran her fingers lovingly over the silver taps attached to the side of the bath. Melissa realized that this meant that she could lie in the bath and control the water flow at the same time and she tingled with excitement. The plug was already in the drain. Turning on the water, she dangled the fingers of her left hand in the flow until the temperature was just right. Not waiting for the tub to fill, she dropped her robe and slipped into the running water.

Trembling with fatigue, she washed the hours of blood and grime and mud and filth from her body. Starting with her feet, she scrubbed every inch of her skin and then moved on to her hair. Sludgy water pooling around her, she pulled the plug and let the remains of her climb swirl away, using her hands to rinse the tub out afterwards. It was only then that she let herself fill the tub again, this time right up to the top. Although her intention was to enjoy a long, leisurely bath, within moments of settling into the warm, clean water she was asleep.

The water had begun to chill when she opened her eyes again. Not ready to get out, she added more hot water. Already having used the sensible soap, she investigated the line of bottles and sponges that sat on the shelf beside the tub. Grapefruit and lemon and jasmine and peaches tickled her nose as she opened the bottles to have a sniff. She tried to remember the smells of her favourite products back home, but couldn't remember them clearly. Even though she had already washed once, she started with her baby toes and worked her way back up again. Finally, smelling of peaches, she sighed and rested her head against the side of the tub. She was clean.

A large squashy chair beside a window beckoned her. Clean and dry and wrapped in the fluffy robe, she tiptoed over to the chair and sat down, tucking her legs under her and leaning against the window ledge. This window was made up of 12 panes of glass that reminded Melissa of an apple pie. Peering through, she expected to see the dark forest beyond, but was surprised to find a garden. A woman sat on the ground in front of the window, pulling weeds out of the soil and putting them in a pile beside her. As Melissa watched, the woman looked up at her and waved. Melissa waved back, feeling again a sense of recognition.

"Are you awake?" The door opened and the old woman entered. Melissa nodded and laughed, knowing full well that she had been asleep. "Well, your clothes are ready. Once you are dressed, come down to the kitchen. You must be hungry." She put the pile of Melissa's clothes on one end of the counter and slipped back out of the room.

The only things Melissa did not put back on were her shoes and socks. Her feet were delighting in freedom, and she couldn't quite bring herself to force them back into the shoes, so she left her shoes and socks neatly outside the bathroom door. The floor was delightfully warm and smooth under her feet, and she didn't think that the owner of this house would mind her going barefoot for a while.

Somehow she already knew the way to the kitchen. At the threshold, she paused. The woman who had greeted her was standing with her back to the door stirring something over the fire. Even though Melissa hadn't noticed before, there was something comforting in the line of her back. Melissa knew her.

"Thank you for drying my clothes," Melissa smiled as she stepped into the room. The woman turned and smiled back.

"It's no problem," she said. "Are you feeling better?"

"Much!" Melissa sighed. "Is there anything I can do to help?"

"Yes, if you don't mind," the old woman said. "Could you bring me in a little more wood for the fire?"

"Of course! Just tell me where to get it," Melissa smiled.

"There will be some just outside the kitchen door," the woman said, pointing in the direction of the door.

Melissa nodded and went outside. The ground outside the kitchen door was hard and well packed with the passage of many feet and felt smooth and soft against her soles. She could see that the forest encircled the garden, but a fence that was covered in climbing flowers and runner beans kept the trees back. Melissa found the wood piled up against the kitchen wall and carried several loads in, being careful not to drop any logs onto her bare feet. When she finished she realized that she had dropped bits of bark and moss onto the floor.

"Have you got a broom I could use to sweep up mess I made?" Melissa asked.

"Of course! It's just tucked away there in the corner," the woman said. "And there is a dustpan beside it!"

Melissa started sweeping up just the mess that she'd made but she soon realized that the whole floor needed to be done. She swept around the cupboards and counters and around the fire, under the table and around the wood that she had just brought in. When the space was clean, she swept the dirt into the dustpan and looked around for a place to put it.

"Just dump it in the fire," the woman said. Melissa emptied the contents of the dustpan onto the flames, causing the fire to falter for a moment. Picking up a couple of logs, she tossed them one after another onto the fire and soon the blaze was crackling cheerfully again. She smiled, dusted off her hands and stood back to admire her handiwork. Turning to speak to the woman, she realized that she was now alone.

"Do you want me to stir the soup?" Melissa called, assuming she had gone into another room or was just outside the back door. There was no answer. The pot that hung over the fire was bubbling merrily and she leaned forward to see what it was. It smelled so delicious her stomach rumbled in response. Finding a stool near the fire, she sat and ran her fingers through her still-damp hair, turning around so that the heat of the fire would dry it. Apart from her hunger, she felt relaxed.

"Oh you are finally here!" A voice broke through her reverie. A woman burst through the kitchen door. "I knew you would make it, but I wondered how long you would be." The woman came and stood in front of Melissa, sticking out her hand for Melissa to shake. "I'm Hortense," she smiled.

"Melissa," Melissa said, shaking her hand.

"Oh, I know who you are. We've been waiting for you," Hortense said with a laugh. Melissa watched her. She had long curly black hair, black eyes and was dressed in black velvet jeans, a white dress shirt and a black leather biker jacket. Her fingernails were painted burgundy and around her neck was a silver necklace made of swirls. She was energy and intensity and didn't fit in this kitchen.

"Why have you been waiting for me?" Melissa asked. Hortense ignored her.

"Isn't supper ready yet?" Hortense asked, leaning over the pot and sniffing its contents.

"I don't think so," Melissa answered. "The woman who was making it has disappeared."

"Well then you'll need to finish! I'm starving."

"Are you sure?" Melissa said, not wanting to interfere.

"Yes! You have a lot of mouths to feed, my friend. You had better get to it." Hortense pulled Melissa to her feet and motioned towards a covered bowl that was sitting by the hearth. "You get started on this, I'll be back in a few minutes."

Melissa stood staring at the place where Hortense had been. Not knowing what else to do she lifted the towel from the top of the bowl and found a ball of risen bread dough. The smell of yeast took her right back to her grandmother's kitchen.

"Punch it down," she heard her grandmother say. Rummaging through the cupboards until she found a container full of flour, Melissa couldn't believe she remembered what to do. Sprinkling the flour on the table, she punched the dough down and then dumped it from the bowl onto the counter. Pulling the dough over towards her, folding it over and then pushing it away again, she kneaded it for several minutes. Four greased and floured loaf pans sat waiting on the counter beside her, so she divided the dough into four pieces and shaped them to fit the pans. Placing one piece into each pan, she put the pans in front of the fire to rise again and covered the loaves with the towel.

Turning her attention to the contents of the pot, she stirred it with the wooden spoon and brought a little bit out so that she could give it a taste. It was a rich stew, filled with vegetables. She tasted it again. What did it need? She thought back again to her grandmother's kitchen, wishing she could remember what ingredients her grandmother had used in her stews.

"First you put the denser vegetables in because they take a long time to cook," Melissa heard her grandmother say. "Things like potatoes and carrots." Melissa smiled at her memories. Turning away from the fire to see what other ingredients she could find, she found she was not alone. To her shock, her grandmother herself stood at the counter behind her, cutting up green beans.

"You need to put the more delicate vegetables in just before you serve it," her grandmother said. Melissa's heart beat erratically in her chest, and she wondered whether she was hallucinating. Of all of the weird things that had happened to her on this journey, this one was the hardest one for her to understand.

"I'm just going to pop outside and see if I can't find some thyme," Melissa heard another voice say. Turning away, she found her granny standing at the door. Granny was her father's mother. She felt Melissa's eyes on her and turned to look.

"Oh honey, you look a bit pale, are you alright?" She asked, guiding Melissa to a chair. Melissa stared at her face, trying to understand what she was seeing. "Oh Madelyn, I think she's coming down with something," she said, turning to Melissa's other grandmother who dried her hands on a tea towel and came over to place a cool palm on Melissa's forehead.

"No," she smiled into Melissa's eyes. "I think that she's just a bit overwhelmed by all of this, aren't you sweetie?" Melissa nodded dumbly.

"Eleanor, when you get that thyme, will you bring in a few handfuls of peas?" Madelyn asked. "They are so lovely and fresh right now, it'll be nice to throw them in at the end." Eleanor nodded her agreement and slipped outside.

"Melissa, come over here and help me cut up these beans," Madelyn said, gesturing with her knife. Melissa had tears in her eyes as she watched her grandmother show her exactly how to cut the beans so that they would be in bite-sized pieces. She realized as she watched that they had the same hands. Her grandmother squeezed her close with one arm.

"Here now, what's all the fuss?"

"It's just nice to see you," Melissa smiled through her tears.

"What are you talking about? I'm always with you," Madelyn said, touching the end of Melissa's nose affectionately. "We all are." She smiled at Melissa's puzzled expression.

"Something smells good!" A voice broke the spell. Another woman came through the door from the hallway. Melissa made a small, strangled cry in her throat and flew across the room and into the arms of her mother.

"Here now, what's wrong?" Her mother asked, pushing the hair back from Melissa's flushed cheeks.

"She's a bit overwhelmed today," Madelyn said.

"It's just so good to see you all," Melissa choked through her tears. Her mother steered her back to the chair. Melissa sat down and just watched as the two women continued to prepare dinner. Amazed at how physically alike they were, she looked down at her own body. She looked at the thighs and the belly that she had always hated because they were not small and slim. Watching these two beloved women, she realized that her body looked a lot like theirs. How could she have missed it before? How could she have hated something that they had given her? Her grandmother bent to put the loaves into the oven, and Melissa was glad she had remembered how to put them on to rise.

Her granny came back through the door carrying a basket of peas and a couple of sprigs of thyme. Melissa watched her with interest as her granny spoke with her mother. They laughed at a shared joke, and Melissa saw her own raised eyebrows on her granny's face. They had the same expressions. How could she never have noticed that?

"Melissa, could you go out and get us some parsley from the garden?" Her mother smiled. Melissa was worried that if she left they wouldn't be there when she got back, but she nodded and got up from the table. It wasn't until she got there that she realized that she couldn't remember what parsley looked like, so she wandered around the rows of vegetables and herbs for a few minutes.

"What are you looking for?" A voice interrupted her search. Another woman was standing in the next row. Her hands were on her hips and she wore a wide brimmed hat to keep the sun from her face. She looked familiar.

"I was sent out for some parsley," Melissa said.

"Is Madelyn making stew?" The woman asked.

"Yes," Melissa nodded.

"The parsley is over on the other side of the herb garden," the woman said. "Come this way." When she turned and walked away along the row, Melissa realized that she was looking at the same back she had seen twice inside the house. This woman had the same shape as her mother and her grandmother. At the other end of the herb garden, the woman bent down to cut a few leafy stems from a small plant. When she turned to give Melissa the small bunch of parsley, Melissa caught her breath, knowing why she recognized her. On her grandmother's mantelpiece had once sat a grainy black and white picture. Melissa remembered the picture and realized that she was now talking to her great grandmother. Not knowing what to say, Melissa stood staring in the gathering darkness. Her great grandmother just smiled at her and turned back to her gardening.

For a long time, Melissa didn't move. Unsure of what to do next, she stared at the forms of the other women in the garden and wondered who they were and whether each of them was one of her relatives. Fighting the urge to run up and hug all of them, she looked down at the parsley she held squashed in her palm and decided to go back inside.

The aroma of baking bread and fragrant stew filled the kitchen. Melissa stood in the doorway and watched her mother and grandmothers as they cooked together. Coming out of shock, she joined the other women at the counter. Her mother showed her how to cut the parsley into very small pieces, and they added it to the stew together. When the bread was ready, Melissa was the one to take it out of the oven. She carried the pans to the windowsill to cool for a few minutes before she gently turned the loaves out onto a rack to cool some more. Her grandmother put a pile of plates onto the table while her granny cut the loaves into slices. They all chatted as they worked.

"Here Melissa, you help yourself to some stew," her mother said, pressing a bowl into her hands.

"Oh, I don't need to go first," Melissa protested.

"Yes, you do," her mother said firmly and calmly. Melissa didn't argue. She was hungry and the stew and the bread smelled incredible. Helping herself to a large spoonful, she took a slice of bread and sat down at the table. The other women continued to bustle around the kitchen while Melissa ate. Enjoying the food almost as much as she enjoyed listening to the conversation going on all around her, Melissa basked in the surrounding warmth. Using her last piece of bread to wipe the last of the stew from the bottom of the bowl, she popped it into her mouth and sighed with delight and satisfaction.

The kitchen was silent. Melissa froze. The other women were nowhere to be seen. The food and the bread and the plates and even her bowl had disappeared. The fire still burned brightly, but there was no evidence of the meal or of the preparation.

"No!" Melissa cried, leaping out of her seat and racing to the counter and to the door and back again. "NO!" She collapsed into tears. If she had known it was all going to be over so soon, she would have done everything she could to keep it going. She would have made that bowl of stew last forever.

"How was supper?" Hortense asked brightly, appearing at the door again.

"Where are they?" Melissa demanded, raising a tear stained face to look at Hortense. "Where are they?"

"They're here. They are all around you," Hortense smiled, sitting in a chair across from Melissa.

"No they're not. I can't see them anymore," Melissa said wearily. "Please, I just want to see them for a moment more. I just want to thank them for everything."

"I can do better than that," Hortense smiled. "Come with me." Melissa wiped tears from her cheeks as she followed Hortense into the twilight. At first she couldn't see why Hortense had brought her out here. Hands on hips, she looked to Hortense for an answer but the woman just smiled and walked further into the garden.

"I told you we were all with you," her grandmother's voice shook Melissa out of her gloom. Her mother and grandmothers stood around her, encircling her in their arms. After a moment, her mother took Melissa firmly by the shoulders.

"But you need to remember how important you are," her mother said, looking her straight in the eye. "You carry all of us. You carry our burdens, our hurts, our triumphs and our joys. What is up to you is which of those things you hold onto, which ones you heal and which ones you leave for the next generation to deal with." Melissa looked at her mother with her eyes full of questions. With a smile, her mother raised her arm and gestured behind her. One step behind her stood Melissa's grandmother and her granny, who turned their heads to look behind them, showing Melissa an unending line of women stretching backwards through time. Her heart knew them all, and she was held in theirs.

"Don't forget about us," a voice said, breaking through the spell. Shock didn't stop her from flinging herself into the embrace of the speaker. It was her grandfather.

"We're holding you too," he said, his voice full of love. Melissa sobbed as she held onto his chest, inhaling the familiar smell. He smelled like work and fresh air.

"You're a pretty special girl you know," he whispered so that only she could hear the words. She clung to him for a moment longer before he gently let go and took two steps backwards.

Melissa's tears continued to fall as her father joined them. Embracing him with all of her strength, she let herself disappear into the love that surrounded her.

Letting go and taking a step backwards, her father glanced over his shoulder, smiling at someone. And then Melissa could see them too. An unending line of men stood behind her father, leading back through time, holding her in their hearts, just like her grandmothers were. Melissa stood facing all of them, not knowing what to do. Reflected in their eyes and the lines of their faces and bodies, she could see something of herself in all of them.

Pain and love and suffering and joy and regret and excitement and passion radiated from the lines of people. Realizing that they had all lived and breathed and laughed and had a hand in creating her, Melissa knew she needed to honour their gifts to her somehow, and she had to take her place in the line. In the quiet, Melissa heard her heartbeat and knew exactly what to do next.

"Let's dance," she said quietly.

The drumming of her heart got louder and louder in her ears until it escaped from her body and joined with the heartbeats of her ancestors. As one, they began to dance. Swirling and swaying and moving her hips Melissa wandered up and down the lines of her ancestors, wanting to pull all of the energy of the dance into herself. She had never allowed herself to dance with them, with her body, or with the world before this moment. A stirring began deep in her belly that she had never felt before. Legs and arms and hips took on a life of their own and, for a moment, Melissa was lost in the energy of the dance. Her ancestors were not old or dead or forgotten; they were right there beside her. They were pure energy and love, and she realized that she was one of them.

One by one her companions slipped away into the darkness until she was standing alone in the moonlight. Face glistening with tears and love, she looked to the sky and smiled.

"I told you we were all here with you," a voice behind her said. Her grandparents stood in the doorway of the house, welcoming her inside. Her grandfather put a few pieces of wood on the fire while Melissa and her grandmother pulled two chairs closer to its warmth. They sat together by the fire, Melissa with her head resting on her grandmother's knee and her hand in her grandfather's. She listened as they told her stories about her roots. She tried to stay awake, but the crackling of the fire was making her sleepy. Their hands, soft and warm on her hand and her head were the last things she felt as she slipped away from them into sleep.

Chapter Twenty

"**A**re you awake?"

Melissa blinked her eyes in confusion. Was she awake? And who had asked her that question? She had no memory of going to bed but she was neatly tucked into bed in a room with tree roots as a ceiling.

"Are you awake?" Hortense peered around the door. "Good. Come on, it's time to get you moving again. We can't stay here in the roots forever!"

"What's next?" Melissa asked, getting up and pulling on her clothes.

"Wings," Hortense laughed.

The fire had burned through the night so they were able to make themselves tea. Strawberries and cherries and raspberries, warm with sunshine filled bowls for breakfast. In one corner of the garden a large apple tree grew heavy with fruit. Melissa picked one fresh, red apple from the tree and whispered her thanks. The tree rustled in reply.

Hortense led the way up five flights of stairs. Melissa kept looking around her and trying to understand where they were. The higher they climbed the less anything made sense. At the top of the seventh flight, Melissa stopped for a moment to catch her breath, hoping they had reached the top. Hortense pulled on a thick rope hanging from the ceiling and a ladder dropped down in front of them.

"I'll go first," Hortense said, setting her foot on the bottom rung. Melissa didn't mind one bit. The space at the top of the ladder was completely dark. Hortense's velvet-clad legs disappeared into the hole, but no light came on, and there was no sound from above. Melissa waited for a moment but Hortense did not reappear or call to her. With no other choice, Melissa climbed the ladder.

Light and air were waiting for her at the top. Far from a dark hole, the top of the ladder leaned against the arms of the tree. Bark scratched at Melissa's arms, and she wobbled a little as she found her balance on a huge limb. A few feet away, Hortense beckoned her through the door of a tiny treehouse.

The ceiling of the treehouse was made of branches of the tree tightly woven together to make a living roof. Melissa merely glanced up at it for a moment as she followed Hortense across the room. Built over and around more branches, the floor was uneven and needed her attention so she didn't fall. It wasn't until they stopped that Melissa realized she could hear whispering. Although they were inside, the leaves above their heads rustled as if in a breeze. Looking up, she smiled as she realized that it was not only leaves overhead, there were also seeds. 'Tree propellers,' her father had called them when she was a child. She remembered picking them up and tossing them in the air to watch as they spun wildly to the ground. Absently, she reached up to pick one from the branch.

"Careful!" Hortense shouted at her. "Melissa, stop." Melissa stood with her hand in the air. The whispering intensified. "Have you really looked at what is around you?" Hortense scolded gently.

Melissa was puzzled, but she looked more closely at the branches above her. With a small cry, she realized that what she had thought were seeds were actually hundreds of pairs of wings. At first she assumed they were butterflies, but she soon realized that they did not have bodies attached to them. Her breath caught as she looked around in awe, and when she exhaled, they rustled in the slight movement of air.

"What..." Melissa couldn't articulate the questions that were filling her head. Tiny and well camouflaged, many of the wings blended into the leaves surrounding them. On closer look, however, Melissa could see that there were other wings hanging in corners and higher up that did not blend in at all. Slowly and carefully, she walked through one room and into the next. This room had two windows at the far end. The closer they got to the window, the bigger and more colourful the wings got. A snowy white pair hung in front of her, and when she reached out and gently stroked the feathers, they rustled in reply. Some wings looked as if they had come from birds, some from butterflies and others looked like they belonged to dragonflies or bumblebees. A shiny pair as black as raven's wings hung beside a delicate iridescent green set. As she walked, some of them brushed against her shoulders, but others remained folded as if in sleep.

"Hortense, what is this place?" Melissa whispered.

"It doesn't have a name," Hortense said. "It's just the place where the wings wait to be assigned."

"Assigned?" Melissa looked at her in confusion. "Do you mean to the animals and birds and insects?"

"No, they have their own waiting area," Hortense smiled. "These wings are for humans."

"Humans!" Melissa shrieked, causing the wings around her to rustle in distress.

"Yes, humans," Hortense said. "Can't you feel yours?"

"Mine?" Melissa laughed. "I don't have any wings."

"Yes, you do. Everyone has them," Hortense shrugged, as if it were the most obvious answer.

"Okay, now I know this is all a dream," Melissa said. I have known my back for a long time now, and I have never seen or felt wings there."

"Ah, but you obviously have never tried then," Hortense smiled. "They are your sacred birthright. They are your connection to your own power, your feminine power. Trust me, if you try to find them, they will be there."

"But you said everyone had them," Melissa protested. If it is a connection to the feminine, does that mean men don't have them? I haven't seen any men on my journey."

"No, men have them too," Hortense smiled. "But they have their own lessons to learn before they find them. Men need to connect to their masculine power before they connect to the feminine, and then the paths can begin to cross."

"What do I do to find my wings?" Melissa asked, looking around the room. "Are mine hanging here?"

"Oh no," Hortense smiled. "These wings are waiting for their owners to begin their journey. Yours have been with you ever since you were a baby. What exactly do you think your shoulder blades are for anyway?"

"I really don't understand," Melissa felt fear rising in her throat. She knew what it was and allowed it out in a small wail.

"Sit still and close your eyes," Hortense said gently. "Just sit quietly for a moment and concentrate on your shoulder blades. Can you feel them?" Melissa nodded.

Melissa sat very still and thought about her shoulders. Tiny voices in her head told her how absurd all of this was, but she gently told those voices to be quiet and kept concentrating. She was surprised to find that she could feel something happening on her back. Breathing deeply, she tried to relax her shoulders as much as possible. Her eyes flew open in surprise. She could feel them. She couldn't see them, but she knew without a doubt that they were there.

"Now all you have to do is concentrate and you can unfurl them," Hortense grinned. Melissa closed her eyes again and concentrated. In her mind, she could see her wings on her back. They were rolled up tightly next to her skin. Gently, she allowed her mind to coax them to unfurl. Tentatively at first, they began to move, and then they rolled open until they were spread out fully across her back, taking up space in the room. Melissa opened her eyes. She didn't need to look in any mirror to know that they were there. She knew they were there; she knew they were blue.

"Now that you know that they are there you can't forget them again," Hortense said. "You can find and unfurl them any time you like, but they are always there with you."

Melissa closed her eyes and visualized folding her wings. It made her smile to know that they were there. Something deep inside her changed in that moment, and she would never be the same.

"It's time for the next step," Hortense smiled. Melissa followed her through the whispering wings to the windows. "It's time for you to decide where you go from here." One window opened back into the forest and the other opened into her apartment. It had been so long since she had thought about home, it took Melissa a moment to recognize her own space.

"I don't understand," Melissa said, looking through both windows.

"You have to choose whether you keep going up the mountain or whether you stop here. You can take all you have learned and go home, or you can keep going and see what is at the end of the journey."

"But I am afraid," Melissa whispered. "I am afraid of both decisions."

"Well that's no excuse," Hortense laughed. "Everyone's afraid. As long as you are alive you will have fear. What matters is how you respond to it."

"But I don't know if I can," Melissa began.

"Oh Melissa," Hortense sighed in exasperation. "Don't you get it yet?"

"Get what?" Melissa asked.

"How powerful you are?"

Melissa stopped and looked at Hortense in shock. Her legs gave away under her and she fell to the floor, watching scenes from her life flick through her brain like index cards in a box. Tears flowed as she realized how much time she had wasted feeling powerless. When she looked back at her life, she could see how truly powerful she had been without even realizing it.

"I'm sorry," she whispered. She was speaking as much to herself as she was to Hortense.

"You don't have to be sorry," Hortense said gently. "Everything you did got you here. You did the best you could in those moments. Guilt and regret have no place in a life that is powerful. What matters is where you go from here."

"Where do I go from here?" Melissa asked.

Hortense threw back her head and laughed. The sound filled the room and all of the spaces that were left around Melissa's heart.

"Well, if you are waiting for a 'happily ever after,' you are not going to get it." Hortense said. There is no ending to this journey. You are going to keep moving whether you go out and greet your life or not. I am not going to tell you what the next step is; you already know what to do next. Melissa, we all carry darkness inside us. Every single one of us is afraid. What matters is not that you make a huge leap, what matters is that you do the best you can. What matters is that you are willing to stand on the edge of every small step and take it. What matters is that you stand at the edge and say 'yes!' to your adventure. Live your life Melissa. Don't wait for it to live for you."

"I want to finish climbing the mountain," Melissa said quietly.

"Pardon?" Hortense said. Melissa smiled and stood up straight.

"I want to finish climbing the mountain. I want to finish what I started."

Without another word, Hortense threw open the window that led into the forest. Melissa walked to the threshold and found that it was not a window at all: it was a door. No longer in the treetops, or even in the forest, a path led from the door straight up to the top of the mountain. Melissa had nearly reached the top without even realizing she was climbing.

Turning to thank Hortense, the only company she found was the whispering wings. Closing her eyes just to make sure that her own were still there, she walked through the door and back onto the path, letting her wings unfurl in joy. Only once did she turn to see how far she had come. In the distance she could see the places she had visited and the thin snaking line of the route she had taken. Laughter trailed behind her as she realized that everything she could see made sense now. Every step had been a part of the climb.

The air was clean and clear. A bird flew overhead, thrilling her with its call. Sitting cross-legged on a rock, she felt the breeze tickle her arms and dance with her hair. The mountain had been climbed. There, at the top, she was alone. She had found only herself. Eyes closed, she enjoyed the feeling of accomplishment for a few more minutes. When she opened them again, she took in the view. Breathing deeply, she shielded her eyes with one hand and turned her body to view as much of the horizon as she could without getting up. Then she stopped and her heart started drumming. In the distance she could see another mountain. It was even higher than this one.

With a knowing deep in her chest, she stood up. Taking one last loving look at the view, she took a step forward. Dozens of different paths started in front of her, all leading in some way towards the next mountain. Thinking of Selene's map, Melissa chose the one that felt right. Remembering what Hortense had told her, she stood right at the edge of the path and put her hands on her hips.

"YES!" She cried, and began walking.

She had not gone very far when the path took her back into the woods. At first the way was clear and she did not worry that she couldn't see where she was going, but then the path narrowed and the way became tangled. Despite concentrating on her feet, Melissa soon lost the path completely. Standing still, she wondered whether she should retrace her steps to find out where she had gone wrong. Before she could turn around, she heard something. Underneath the sounds of the birds and the trees, was a low, rhythmic vibration. Knowing now that everything that appeared to her was meant for her, Melissa followed the noise. Pushing through the tangled undergrowth, she allowed the sound to lead her through the trees and into a large clearing.

Her heart knew what was going on before her eyes did. Women of all shapes and sizes and colours moved before her, their own hearts beating together as one. From all sides of the clearing more women were leaving the woods and joining them. Melissa noticed that the women were actually holding hands and travelling in one long continuous line, spiralling in towards the middle of the space. She couldn't see the end, but she knew that if she joined these women that she would eventually find the centre. Compelled forward, Melissa joined the end of the line. She wasn't at the end for long, for it was only a few moments before another woman held her other hand. In one long line they walked, circling in from all sides of the forest, all pulling towards the centre.

Melissa held tightly to the hands of the women on each side of her. Power and energy radiated from them and she realized that she was radiating the same power. She felt it in her bones and in her blood, but more than that she felt it in the space they held between them. She knew it was that space that was more important than anything. Spinning inwards, she drew closer and closer to the centre.

Melissa blinked. She was standing on a city street. Not understanding where she was, she assumed that she was about to learn another lesson. As she tried to get her bearings, the street began to look familiar. Nestled between two shop fronts, the building in front of her had a dark green door. Unlike its neighbours, the door had a round silver spiral on it instead of a number. Melissa stared at the door for a moment and then looked down at her feet. She was wearing a pair of sparkly red heels.

"Are you awake?" Melissa looked around for the person speaking. A woman stood beside her.

"I'm sorry to bother you, but I am trying to find this place," the woman said, holding out a business card. Melissa looked at the card in her hand and suddenly she understood.

"Yes," Melissa smiled. "It's just there, but you might have to walk down the street again before you can see it." The woman looked puzzled and walked away.

Melissa looked down at her feet again and back up at the door. It was gone.

"Are you awake?" The woman's question echoed in her head. Feeling in her pocket, she touched the little seed that nestled there and then she shrugged her shoulders just to make sure. Relief made her grin: her wings were still there. Turning her back on the buildings, she walked down the street towards home.

"Yes, I am," she laughed.

THE END

18223328R00130

Made in the USA
San Bernardino, CA
04 January 2015